*About THE STAR MILL:*

Like *SAGA OF LOST EARTHS* this science-fantasy was inspired by the little-known Finnish Epic, the *KALEVALA*. But its stage is not simply a North European peninsula and a folk who put a new word of courage into the warring world—*sisu*—a land of sunlit lakes and forests during the months of all-summer, of howling flint-starred skies in the all-dark; like the music of the Finnish titan, Jean Sibelius, and the godfraught dreams spun around those ancient fires, it presumes to reach out to far stars, to include even the Powers that cause what is to be.

Wondersmith Hero Ilmarinen fashioned a Sampo of infinite power. The Star-Witch of Pohyola twisted its atom-shuffling power to destroy and not recreate. There will be no end to this destruction until all matter, animate and inanimate, has been shattered. Through endless generations the Vanhat must wait until a new hero can be reassembled out of ancestral crumbs of heroic power, gene by gene. For it shall be he and he alone who can become the starpower axis that can destroy the destroyer.

—Emil Petaja

# THE
# STAR
# MILL

by

EMIL PETAJA

ACE BOOKS, INC.
1120 Avenue of the Americas
New York, N.Y. 10036

*Cover by Jack Gaughan*

To

SIME and SENIA

PART ONE

## THE DERELICT

"Then did Pohyola's old Mistress
Speak aloud the words of portent:
'Still can I devise a method,
'Gainst thy ploughing and thy sowing,
'Gainst thy children and their children . . .'"

KALEVALA: *Runo XLIII*

# I

First awareness of existence as a living organism brought him only the symptom of pain. Pain pinned down his skull. Pain twisted his nerves. Pain shuddered down the length of his long body. It was as if this lithe, well-muscled form that was suddenly *him* had been carelessly flung onto the rocky surface like a piece of galactic debris.

This must be the way one is born. An abrupt wrench, and this wretched chunk of matter suddenly possesses sentience. Unwillingly. Pell-mell. Only *he* was born with the potential to understand that it happened.

He forced open his eyes. That simple act of his eyelids' muscles caused hideous pain. But here he was, shivering from the mauling pain, and he must force his senses to take account, one by one.

He looked up.

He shivered harder. Up there was raw black space. He lay very still, staring up into it with horror. Those needles driving down on him were stars, unnaturally bright because there was no atmosphere of any kind between him and them. Inside his cells something recoiled, whimpering. It didn't want to be born. It didn't want the pain of being alive.

Time lashed him, changing him from baby to boy in seconds. Then, more slowly, a man. . . .

He found a voice in himself. He groaned. Now an arm trembled up along the metallic suiting that protected his sudden body from the deadly cold of space and provided it with air. His gloved fingers explored him; they discovered that a plastic helmet bulbed out around his head, noting with some interest the phenomenon of the glove flattening out inches from his eyes.

He was learning, in spite of the pain. By winces he worked up to a sitting position. Little by little he took inventory. Of himself. Of his surroundings.

The rock on which he had been flung must be some kind of asteroid. Some small mote or dust-fleck out in the endless gaping maw of deep space. The inverse curve of skyline told him the rock was small. And something more subtle, some intuitive knowledge thrusting out of his cells, told him that he was quite, quite alone on it.

He shook uncontrollably for a long minute, looking up at those mocking winks of light far above. Hungrily his eyes moved along the perimeter of the effulgent corona of reflected starlight for some scrap of himself. Of *Man*. But there was nothing. No Ship. No empty food container. Nothing. Not a hint that anyone besides him existed anywhere in the universe.

He retreated back into his pain.

Why did he hurt?

Spastic muscular contortion brought some answers. He inferred that before he had been flung onto the rock he had been savagely beaten. There were long welts and sore bruises on his muscular arms and legs. His face hurt, too. It had been a hand-to-hand battle, without the suit, of course. He had fought his enemy with every shred of his youthful strength.

And he had won!

He had defeated his enemy, by physical force or mental agility and—miraculously—somehow pulled himself into the spacesuit he was wearing, escaping to this rock. Yes. The enemy had *not* put him there. That must be it. He had escaped this far; either his enemy could not follow him, or didn't bother, assuming that he would die here within a short time.

Which, of course, he would.

Meanwhile—

"Who—" He staggered up on his feet, pivoting his face at those mocking far-off suns and yelling:

*"Who am I? Who am I?"*

The stars burned coldly down. They were indifferent to him and his pitiful existence. These small creatures that moved briefly among them were of measureless insignificance. This one was no better than the rest. Let him shout. Soon he would die from lack of air, water, food. So what?

Or—was it possible that something or someone up there in all that vacancy cared? Hope flickered, died.

Time went. The stars moved on their paths. The little asteroid did its part in the intricate cosmic mobile.

Sometimes he went on a ramble across the broken metallic rock. His wounds hurt less but his mental agony grew and grew. There was water in the suit's canteen, enough for perhaps two weeks. There was capsulated food in the wide black belt. The suit itself kept him warm. But the emptiness in his brain, the oblivion that ought to have been memory, crushed most of his instinct to survive.

*Lie down and die.*

He found a rocky outcrop, curled up, waited.

# THE STAR MILL

Bitterness tormented him. His body told him he was young. He didn't want to die. Especially he didn't want to die not knowing what he was all about.

Hunger stretched his belly. His lips cracked like small deserts. The heat-power in his suit began to fail; his fingers and toes went numb.

Death clawed down. Up in the blackness stars started to form designs. Patterns, as if they wanted to tell him something. Maybe it was the cold, the thirst, the hunger. Yes. His drained mind was beginning to make its own wild fantasies. There were three of them. Three heroic giants striding down out of the windows in the sky. One young, careless: golden blond hair framed a handsome laughing face. One old: the beard lying against his deep blue tunic was white as a swan; the combed brown face was stern in prodigious thought. One lanky and in-between, with his pointed chin and his wide mouth decorated by a crop of copper-red hair like ornamental twists of wire.

He stared at the heroic figures while the space-cold cut through his veins. They seemed about to speak but a roar of thunder inside his brain smashed back their words. The hand of death scraping his eyes tore them away; the sky was empty and black again.

He shrank against the icy rock, mumbling.

Now, whether from inside the bolted chambers of his mind or from that black starless patch to his left, came a harsh, gleeful cackling laugh. It teased his dying consciousness. It spun from out of that black nebular patch, hovering just over his head. The cackler was insane, invisible—and triumphant.

He lifted a few inches. It took every shred of strength left in his half-frozen body.

*"Autta!"*

The plea bubbled out of cold-locked jaws.

9

Death visions tortured him again. He saw a wide black lake and a black swan swimming majestically through blue mists, singing. He saw a girl with auburn hair and green eyes that wept uncontrollably—for him. Shafts of silver light seemed to stab his retreating mind. A clap of cosmic thunder shattered the galaxy.

"Ukko!"

Again the overwhelming vibration like thunder.

*I AM HERE.*

A crack opened in his locked mind. He glimpsed a wide snow-blanketed valley, a clutch of brown log huts, and, beyond the dark green forest path, a lake. Thunder rolled benevolently down from the high crags that completely surrounded the woodsmoke misted valley.

*I AM HERE, SON OF ILMARINEN.*

Then:

Sudden, utter silence. Silence like the end of all that has been, is, or will be.

Beyond his consciousness something told him that this was personal death. But what was that curious buzzing noise? It nagged down into the abyss he was halfway down, coaxing his dead senses back to life. It overcame his pleasant wish for extinction.

Voices. Random voices, exploding in excited meaningless phrases. The audio within his suit, activated automatically by transmission from within its acceptance radius, was pulling in sound.

"Good God, it *is* a man! I saw him move!"

"How the hell did he get way out *here*, Captain? This sector of *Ursae Majoris* is nowhere, man!"

"Poor bastard, we've got to pick—"

"No . . . Too close to the Storm . . . We're not sure what he is."

"Could be a Mocker."

"*Naw*—that war is over, man!"

"Shall we break out the lifeboat, Captain Grant?"

"No."

"Hell! We can't just sail off and leave the poor—"

"Yes, we can."

"No, Captain! We just can't!"

"We can. We're too close to the Black Storm."

"But not inside it. Lord, Cap—"

"No."

"Excuse me, Captain Grant, but I feel that all three of us have a say in this. It's a man's life."

"Brooks is right, Cap. If we pull out, all our lives we'll sweat blood from wondering whether . . ."

"A vote, Captain Grant! Let's vote on it!"

"No. Absolutely no. I am captain on my ship and my job is to protect my crew, even from themselves. I know just how you feel. I'm human, damn it! I'm as curious as both of you are to know what that derelict is all about. I've been a starman for twenty-nine years. I know how you feel. It's a long pull between anything habitable out here. Every human life is like gold."

"Then put it to a vote! McGinn and I'll sign anything you want us to releasing you from responsibility. Hurry! Can't you see he's dying?"

## II

HE AWOKE alone, alone in a small metal cubicle. It was so small that the wall above his bunk had a twenty-degree curve to it. He hurt in various places, so he knew he hadn't died on the rock; his spacesuit had been removed along with his claw-raped tunic, which had been replaced with a close-fitting gray uniform. For a while he just lay there, wary and taut. Beneath him thrummed motors of some kind; he was aware by instinct or cellular familiarity of thrust, movement.

He was on a spaceship. A small starship.

He blinked down at the long limbs attached to a flat-belly torso. This was *him*. He was young, strong, alert. But who in the hell was he?

With a silent swift movement he slid down off the bunk. He found some boots near the foot of the anchored bunk; he put them on. Thoughts began to crystallize. He remembered the rock and the weird visions when the creeping cold took over. What had happened next? Oh, yes. The voices on the audio. So they had voted to save him, in spite of the Captain's demurs. The other two members of the small starship had won out. They had picked him up, fed and doctored him, then left him alone to sleep off the effects of exposure and exhaustion. How long? No telling.

He tried his legs. They worked fine. His muscles creaked and his sore spots twinged, but he was a functional organism again, whole and ready. Ready for what?

"*Who am I?*" His voice was a raw whisper across the ten-foot cubicle.

Whirling toward the closed hatch he saw that it had a long mirror set in it. Forcing his fists to uncurl, his legs to relax their fighting stance, he moved to the mirror.

He stared in.

Who . . . ?

Anyway, not a two-headed monster. He saw a human face: long, narrow, saturnine. Hollow caves. The dour, sardonic cast of it was relieved somewhat by a generous mouth with uptilted laugh creases—and a ragged copper-wires beard! He wasn't pretty, for a fact. The face had character and a kind of amiability, but the planes were too sharp, the cheekbones too prominent. The hungry gauntness wore the ragged copper-red moustache and beard with a kind of joviality, matched by keen deep blue eyes that wore over them heavy thatches of that same flamboyance.

There was something else. He moved closer to the mirror.

Across his left cheek, flaming off an overlong red sideburn down to less than an inch from his wide mouth, was an angry crimson scar, shaped like a scimitar.

He stared at the scar and something inside of him went ice-cold. It was like a brand. He was branded, marked like a leper or—

The hatch opened cautiously, putting the scar reflected in its mirror closer to him.

"You're awake?"

He stepped back so that the youngster poking his dark head in could move all the way in. He closed the hatch behind him, quickly and furtively. His wide-nosed face split a grin.

"I'm Joe McGinn. First Mate, it says on my stripe. Actually, on one of these X-Plor mosquitoes First Mate means everything down to chief cook and lav scrubber." He held out a plastic mug that steamed with inky liquid. "Brought you some coffee. That's the first thing I want when I wake up. You?"

The monosyllabic inquiry included quite a bit more. First Mate Joe McGinn's Black Irish eyes were agog with curiosity about the castaway his vote had helped save.

When the stranger said nothing, he chortled on. "You were out like a light when Brooks and I scooped you into the boat. Cap, that's Captain George T. Grant of T.D.S. X-Plor Fleet, made us jettison your suit and your clothes, just in case. You know. The Black Storm."

He tried. The words that dragged out slowly and awkwardly didn't mean much because there wasn't much conscious memory to back them up. It was almost as if some other language besides universal space-idiom would come easier. Yet he did understand and absorb what Joe McGinn was telling him. He was on one of the small Terran Fleet exploratory vessels, small to conserve fuel for the long time-jumps and for versatility when they found something worth close investigation. Captain George Grant hadn't wanted to pick him up. Brooks, ecology tech and ship's medic, had joined McGinn in overriding the Captain's veto.

His answers to the youngster's curiosity were mostly questions. McGinn obliged. He was a great talker.

"Why'd we do it—pick you up? Hell, new faces are few and far between in this part of Big Ursa. We've been out seven months this time, haven't seen anything even near human until you." He chuckled boyishly. "You know, I'm not supposed to be here. Cap said don't go near the cabin. He's got a bug in his ear about the Storm. That's why he stuck you way down here by yourself."

He held out the steaming mug. "Drink your coffee."

When he reached for it their fingers touched. He pulled the mug and his hand back with a convulsive motion. He wanted to scream at the boy to get the hell out of here. Do what your Captain told you! Keep away! *Don't touch me!*

He didn't, though. He just stood there with the coffee slopping over his shivering hand.

McGinn blinked.

"Hey, you're not in too good shape yet. Better lay down and flake out some more." He opened the door behind him and backed out. "Sorry, fella. You take it easy now."

The hatch slapped briskly shut and there was that copper-decorated face staring at him again, like an accusing ghost. The red scar seemed to blaze in the mirror.

A light insistent tapping pulled him out of nightmarish slumber. The hatch opened on a new face this time. This face wore a transparent helmet over it; the tall man it belonged to wore a metallic suit and gloves. An aquiline nose almost brushed the glasslike curve; it projected down off a high freckled forehead of thinning sandy hair. The smile and the gray eyes were provisionally friendly, courteous, less openly buddy-buddy than young McGinn.

"I'm Jeff Brooks. I run the ecology tests when there's anything to run, which is seldom in these parts. Captain Grant would like a word with you in his cabin if you're up to it."

He nodded and followed the suited figure down the narrow hatchway and up an abrupt metal stairs. Across a catwalk was the Captain's roomy quarters, roomy because it served multiple-duty as chart room and dining room; the half-open door across it gave him a wedged look at the controls deck. McGinn was at the controls. He, like Brooks and the Captain, wore anti-radioactivity gear.

The man who whipped briskly out from behind a wide chart table wore a dapper black Starman's tunic under the transparent r.a. gear. He was below medium height, slim, athletic, military in every gesture. There were patches of white at his temples. His triangular face appeared stiff, almost waxy; only his eyes showed animation, glinting with cold brown fire. He wore all of his ribbons and braid, even on such a long lonely trek.

His brief sharp glance was all-inclusive. After a silent moment his thin tight mouth relaxed and produced a faint smile of welcome.

"I am Captain George Grant."

The derelict nodded. That was the best he could do to acknowledge the introduction. The Captain's graying eyebrows pinched closer.

"How do you feel?" he asked.

"All right."

"Good. Then you can relieve our curiosity a little by telling us who you are, and how you got way off here where, as far as we know, nothing human can exist."

He shrugged. To his right he saw the controls room door open wider under young McGinn's urging boot. All three of them were waiting. Waiting for answers.

"Well?" Grant's voice had a sharp edge now.

"Sorry. I can't tell you. I don't know."

Three assorted involuntary sounds.

"You mean you can't remember anything?" Grant barked. "Not even your name?"

"No. Nothing. I was born on that rock." He brushed his eyes with an angry gesture. "I don't remember a damn thing. Not who I am. Not how I got there. Nothing. My mind is wiped clean." Words tumbled out now. It was some relief to share his torture.

Captain Grant's sharp eyes narrowed thoughtfully. "But you are human."

"Human?" Of course he was human! He bridled back in a rush of furious indignation.

"I am referring to the simulacra we fought during the last years of the Alien Wars. Creatures bred to look and react like humans, manning ships just like ours."

"I'm human!" he shouted.

This time the appraisal was longer, more studied.

"The tests I gave him were all perfect," Brooks put in. "He responded positively to his blood plasma type as well as to the medication."

"So did the Mockers," Grant said dryly. "However, I believe him." He faced his unwanted guest. "Maybe the trauma of being deserted there on that chunk of bare rock, facing certain death, did snap off part of your mind. Maybe you don't know about Man in Deep Space. How, after time-skip took us to the stars, we developed a kind of defensive affinity for our own kind, in spite of the attempts by other intelligent races to trick us. I'm not an esper, but I've been a Starman for almost thirty years and I know what is human and isn't. You might say I can smell it." He allowed his wax-tight jaw to relax a little, then tightened it again. "You are one of us. I accept that. *But what else are you?*"

The long fingers moved involuntarily to the red scar. Grant's scowl deepened.

"You were close to the Storm. For days. Weeks. Lord knows how long or where you were before that. We know that to touch even the fringe area of the Black Storm means instantaneous disintegration, but we don't know anything about what long duration that close could do." His gloved hand clenched and struck the map on the table. "We just don't know!"

The shaggy red head bent down. "You keep talking about the Black Storm—!"

"He needs briefing," Brooks suggested.

"Maybe a shot of recent history might trigger his memory," McGinn piped from the open door.

Captain Grant paced the room with military strides. His apprehension, his distaste, was hidden behind that blank mask, but it was palpable. It crackled the air with every step his polished boots took.

"Amnesia is a convenience, sometimes self-induced. Our Terran Council has had some fantastic dealings with alien devices. For instance, what if you were *put* there on that rock after your mind had been deliberately erased? What if we were intended to find you, take you back to Terra with us?"

Silence, while the significance of the Captain's rhetorical question sank in. He continued:

"The Black Storm was discovered here at the point-star the ancients called Merak in *Ursae Majoris* by roving second-generation colonists less than a century ago. How long it has existed and what it is—we can't even guess. Our newest instruments can't probe deep enough into the swirling nebular mass to compute it with any accuracy. All we know is that at the heart of that black chemical mass of radioactivity is *something*. Something that destroys everything that comes near it. We lost a lot of ships trying to find out what. Starmen are born curious; they can't let well enough alone. We keep losing ships in the Black Storm, year by year. Then there are the cargo ships and private syndicate craft that blunder off course in this frontier area. . . ."

Captain Grant's grim brooding look as he flicked a glance from Brooks toward McGinn at the controls said: *I should have prevented the pick-up if I had to knock your heads together, damn me for a blasted fool!*

Brooks thrust in, out of his bookish studies:

"One theory of the Storm, or Nebula as they call it, for want of specific information, is that it's a radioactive dump. That it was material hauled out into space by some race outside our galaxy and has been drifting deeper into our Milky Way for light-years. Yet, erratic as it is deadly, it has none of the characteristics of a true nebula. Some of our way-out brains go so far as to postulate that the Black Storm is *controlled!*"

"By—who?"

"You tell us," Captain Grant snapped. "Maybe it was sent into our galaxy to soften us up before . . ." He barked a dry laugh. "Hell, this is wild! The Terran Fleet has cut a wide swath; there's a lot of nothing between planetary suns, and nowhere have we discovered any hint of the super-super races our imaginative writers dream up. Everything falls right within the Fleet's calculated potential. Even the Mockers were foreseeable."

Brooks nodded. "Yet the worst feature of the Storm is

that it's growing—and fast! It entraps everything that cuts into its elliptical fringe and reduces it into molecular dust. This dust takes on its characteristic seething menace and expands it. It picks up all manner of space debris, too, barreling along like a black hell-ball." His gray eyes looked at horror. "With all due respect to the Fleet's hands-off policy, something's got to be done about it before long! We have got to probe into its nucleus somehow—or else!"

The man with the copper beard felt a creeping numbness move up from his magnetic boots to his locked brain. McGinn missed a driving meteorite nest, swerved; the ship lurched when the automatics took over and corrected. The three in the master cabin bent like reeds in a high wind. Captain Grant swore and shouted at the First Mate to keep his eyes on the fore-vid.

Captain Grant snapped a look at the copperbeard.

"Well?"

"Sorry. Nothing you've told me helped. I still can't remember a damn thing."

Grant's lips tightened over a stifled rush of words as he went back to his star-maps behind the table. He didn't look up but his hands shook a little at their work.

"May I try, sir?" Brooks asked.

Grant shrugged.

"You're one of us"—the mild-mannered scientist opened —"and of course our hearts are close to Terra. Maybe something more close to home will help. For instance, the World Council. The shielded close-security park area centered at what was once Washington, D. C., where the Council holds its sessions and decides all-important Terran Empire questions. Does that ring a bell?"

"No."

"Except for the extreme Polar areas"—Brooks tried again—"Terra is practically all Cities, numbered Cities, with hundreds of Levels to each City. The Cities are so crowded and similar that the local travel terrans used to indulge in is pointless. And there is a long waiting list for star colonies. X-Plor keeps reaching out further and further in Deep to find habitable planets, but the spaces in between are endless, and usable worlds so pitifully few. Not to mention the incredible expense of getting them there, battling primitives, wedging in a toehold. Still, that's our only hope. The Levels leap higher, or burrow deeper; the lists stretch longer. T.D.S. X-Plors use these 'mosquito' ships for frontier thrusts to conserve fuel for such long pulls. These uncharted stints are hit and miss and"—the sallow face puckered—"starmen don't make very good insurance risks."

He paused hopefully. Captain Grant kept at his work of charting new area.

From his post, McGinn chuckled. "It's a short life; time-skip takes it out of a guy. But it's better than being a sardine buried down in the Levels."

Again that hopeful silence. Nobody looked at the derelict; they just waited for something to develop out of the mental prodding.

He sighed. "Sorry."

"Nothing at all?" Brooks asked, with sympathy.

"Nothing." The red scar flared out under an angry rush of blood. "Why didn't you leave me on that rock? Why take chances?"

Brooks grinned wryly. "I really don't know. I've only been with Captain Grant seven years and this is Joe's first long pull. How do you explain? Deep Space is so big —so frighteningly impersonal—you develop a kind of reverence for any kind of life. You cherish it. Every scrap of humanity becomes important. Joe and I—we just couldn't leave you there. Captain Grant's gone beyond us, developed a kind of defensively reactionary hardness. Joe and I haven't—yet."

Captain Grant's head snapped up.

"I am Captain. This ship has been my heart and my soul for fifteen years, and before that another just about like it. We had our little vote, yes. But it meant nothing! Neither did the responsibility release you two dreamed up." His eyes went from Brooks to the derelict. "We were close to the Storm, not to brush the fringe, but too damn close for comfort. The instruments for measuring radioactivity went ape and they are still ape. God knows why! Maybe it was the dip down to your rock or—"

"Maybe it's me!" He was beyond bitterness by this time. "You should have left me there."

"*Yes!*" Captain Grant went back to work grimly.

"Still," Brooks put in mildly, "our friend here doesn't show any evidence of exposure, at least not—"

"Not yet! But it's a long seven-weeks' haul until we move into our solar system."

"Maybe our techs can learn something from him about the Storm after his memory comes back. Bringing him back to Terra might just be critically important."

"Or lethal," Grant muttered.

The copper wires shifted in a droll attempt at a smile. "How about a name of some kind? I might get tired of being called 'him' or 'that bloody bastard' for seven weeks!"

From the controls, McGinn chirped, "You already got one, pal!"

They turned.

"What do you mean?" Grant cracked.

"Sorry, Cap. Didn't mention it before because you said not to handle anything about Ilmar when we removed and tossed out his gear. I got that little job, as you know, I found a scrap of nameplate in the neckpiece. It was pitted and chewed up, but there was half a name you could read. Ilmar."

The humor lines deepened under the red beard.

"At least I've got a name now. *Ilmar.*"

## III

ILMAR. His first knowledge of a personal identity. Even that wasn't certain; he could have been wearing somebody else's space gear. Still, it was a beginning, and he buffeted it around and around in his mind in the sleepdarks, trying to fashion it into a key that would unlock one of those bolted doors. Sometimes he would leap up from a nebulous nightmare of running, fighting—fighting, fleeing—with a sense of sweating urgency. *There was something that he must do.* Something unendurably significant. Then would drift up a kind of mindless cackling and even that much knowledge was buried again. His stiff muscles would relax a little and off he would go into more enigmatic nightmares.

Came the time when his sudden waking was not sleepmare.

Ilmar bolted up so fast his head struck the curved ceiling over his narrow bunk. It came again, the wild pounding of fists on the cubicle door.

"Ilmar!"

The muffled whisper was Brooks'. It was strangled out of dry desperate horror. Ilmar leaped off the bunk and flung open the hatch. In the half-light the medic's face was ash-gray and twisted.

"What is it?"

"Joe! Little Joe!"

"What—"

"He's—sick." Brooks' shoulders were shaking.

Ilmar was agape with sleep and flaying nightmares. "Sick?" He grabbed for Brooks' rocking shoulders but Brooks leaped back down the corridor with a whimpered cry. He wasn't wearing his r.a. shielding. Ilmar dropped his arm abruptly.

"He wouldn't tell Grant," Brooks sobbed. "Not even me. I'm medic, but he knew it was no use." His wrenched-out words did not accuse Ilmar; they were bitter with grief, no more. "Joe must have been in hell for days. It was his watch, and it must have got so bad he couldn't make it. I put the ship on auto and came looking. I— I found him in the hatchway outside our double cabin. He tried to make it, falling apart as he was—"

Brooks' passion of vomiting sobs shattered away talk. Ilmar knew there was a deep feeling between the men; there had to be out-of-the-ordinary friendship to sustain crewmen, as yet unseasoned as Capain Grant, locked up in a metal can hurtling across haunted voids.

"Did you tell Grant?"

"Not—not yet. Listen! I came to warn you!"

"Warn?"

"Don't you understand? Joe touched your suit, hunting for that nameplate. He came to see you without an r.a. shield. He told me. That's what did it."

Ilmar stared out of hollow dead eyes. Self-horror welled up in his craw, choking away words and thoughts. With effort he forced it away.

"You didn't touch his body?"

"Sure!" Brooks voice rang with defiance. "Sure I did! I couldn't leave him lying there like that. I tried to pull him back up on his bunk but—" Horror overtook him for a few heartbeats. "—Joe f-fell apart. In my hands. His body came to pieces, while part of it was still alive!" He shuddered against the dark wall.

Ilmar brushed past him, careful not to touch him as

they moved down the narrow hatchway. When he saw
the First Mate his neck-muscles became strangling ropes
and it was mercy to turn away and retch.

"He's dead now, thank God," Brooks said, in a kind of
crooning prayer. Then he pulled himself straight. "Listen,
Ilmar—before I tell Captain Grant we've got to get busy.
Get you off the ship!"

"Off the ship!" Ilmar only stared. "What good would
that do? Now?"

"Captain Grant'll burn you, don't you see? And you're
not really to blame! It's not your fault that you're immune
to the Storm! What we've go to do while Captain Grant's
still sleeping is change course. Move out of time-skip.
Find a planet of some kind, or an asteroid. Put you in a
suit and drop you on it in the boat before—"

"Why? Why would you do that?" Ilmar was past car-
ing about himself. He had no personal existence anyway, only a name. He was a breathing, walking horror.
Let Captain Grant use a blaster on him as soon as possible. Burn the malignance he carried with him in one overwhelming burst of sunfire.

"Ilmar! The way I figure it is—you're immune *for a
reason*. Terra must know that reason. The rest of us don't
matter. Hurry! Let's go!"

Ilmar blocked his way to the control room with his
virulent presence. He said it all in one word:

"*No.*"

Staring down at the untidy heap of disintegrating cells
that had once been his hand-picked, likable, impudent
First Mate, Captain Grant's eyes became round chunks
of glacial ice. Brooks was weeping again for his lost
buddy. Ilmar stood aside, watching them gravely, as if
all of this had nothing whatever to do with him. It was
just another of his recurrent nightmares.

Finally Grant's r.a. protected hand moved to close the death-cabin door.

They followed him to main cabin. Brooks checked the controls. Captain Grant stared at Ilmar bleakly.

"Would you prefer to do it yourself?"

Brooks cried: "No!"

"I thought Joe was your friend."

Brooks went into a rapid-fire dissertation about Ilmar being immune and Terran scientists must have the opportunity for discovering why. It was more important than they were, more important than Grant's fanatical devotion to his starship. Grant listened grimly.

"The question is, will we make it to Terra?"

Brooks' face flamed with dedication. Ilmar thought it was that McGinn must not have died for nothing. *They* must not die for nothing. There must be meaning to all of this ravening horror.

Captain Grant whipped behind his desk, checking the ship's course, calculating. His cold-fire eyes moved thoughtfully from Ilmar to Brooks.

"McGinn touched the nameplate. Gloves, but not r.a. He visited Ilmar, unshielded. Naturally he was first to go. So we know the amount of contagion Ilmar carries is very small, in comparison to the instantaneous rubble the ships that hit the fringe become. Maybe it was a random spit tentacle flung out from the ellipse. Who knows? Anyway, the effect's cumulative. And—" His eyes softened on Brooks in ordinary Fleet tunic. "You're next."

Ilmar saw the medic's lips go white.

"Yes," he clipped out. "I shared Joe's cabin. I was careful to keep shielded, as you told us, but—" He held up his bare hands.

Captain Grant went to work, feeding data into the computer in the control wall. "Time," he muttered. "We've got to buy *time!* It's not only us. It's the ship. If the engines get it, or the computer, or the automatics—"

Watching and listening to the two of them discussing their deaths and the ship's death with fine assumed calm, Ilmar found his spectator's indifference drop away. It was sloughed off by a cellular storm spreading out from his groin in all directions, howling through him, tearing his veins and his nerves.

"Maybe you can take it," he muttered. "I can't."

Captain Grant flicked him a waxen glance; Brooks stood across the desk from him like a totem, staring at the winking lights on the computer as its tremendous, condensed brain whipped through the data Grant had fed it.

Ilmar moved; he ran onto the balcony catwalk above the cabins and engine hatches. He lunged down the ladder to the narrow down-corridor to the outside hatch with the red eye on it and the sign lettered in red: DANGER. DO NOT REMOVE CLAMP OR TOUCH LEVER TO AIRLOCK.

Ilmar touched. He snapped back the precautionary clamp over the airlock lever and had the door open, even before the hissing air had filled it. Brooks' awkward tackle caught him while his stringy form was bent and stepping through the oval hatch. He lashed out, but Brooks' sobbing determination spun him down. That he was touching Brooks' bare hands made him shudder. He lay in the curved corner, blinking and swearing.

"All right! *Get away from me!*"

Brooks moved back and reclosed the airlock. A kind of triumph glowed in his scholarly face. "Don't you see, Ilmar? I think we're going to make it!"

Captain Grant's smile, behind the medic, was slightly ghastly. "Yes. The odds are rough, but it's mathematically possible. Brooks is right. The only thing that'll keep us going at this point is getting you back to Terra. Alive."

## IV

ILMAR holed up in his cubicle like a rat. He heard them moving heavy plates of shielding around him and his cell, but he didn't open the hatch except to pick up the tray of food Brooks left there every half day. Guilt rode him through every waking hour and strangled away exhausted sleep with nightmares. He ran down benighted corridors, battering his fists against those iron doors until his hands were ragged stumps. Only once, when he opened the door too soon, did he see Brooks. He wasn't Brooks any more. He was a stalking horror with skeleton hands and wide dead eyes. It was a long time before he opened the door again.

At some nadir stage, when the necessity for relief from the totality of his agony put him on the lip of some bottomless brink, that name rang out across eternity like a great resounding chord of trained thunder.

*Ukko.*

*Ukko.*

It connoted thunder-power, too. Power to help him and all who knew what it meant and how to employ it. Still, mocked a second voice—a hag's cackle—this was all part and parcel of his inexhaustible agony. The torture of hope.

He flailed his body and his brains for more. Something more than this wafted scent of beneficence across the aching void of time and space. There wasn't any more. He lay there in the dark, begging, but nothing happened.

When hunger and thirst demanded it, he crawled off the steel bunk and cracked open the door. Before now when Brooks had brought him his food he gave the hatch a light tap. There had been none in some time; and now there was no tray.

Brooks was dead. That was it. Ilmar saw young Mc-Ginn lying there with his cells oozing away into nothing, and now it had happened to Brooks. How about Captain Grant? Maybe the automatics were moving the starship mindlessly on the way to Terra?

Weak from lack of food, he crumpled. He lay there for a long time, gathering up strength and reason crumbs from out of the dearth. He climbed the steel wall with shuddering fingers, hunting for the light switch. He found it; it snapped on just for one good look before it went out again.

His cracked lips let out a yell at what he saw. The room! The walls! While he had been lying there in the dark a stealthy paced horror had been at work. The metal walls were eaten away in great ragged holes; in other places were angry pits like metallic acne scars, a touch and the bleached steel would crumble away in fine powder. While he had lain there all that time, helplessly reproaching his existence, this had happened. The horror in him was relentlessly taking over the ship, as it had taken human flesh.

He clawed up on his feet and backed out into the corridor. Here the walls were pitted but wholesale destruction had not yet begun. He staggered down the companionway on unsteady feet. He reached the up-ladder to the metal balcony and the master cabin. His fingers closed on the railing.

"Stay where you are, Jonah!"

Grant's voice was a feral snarl. Ilmar stayed where he was; he blinked up. He cracked an admiring grin at what the Captain had done. Besides shielding Ilmar's central cubicle to protect the vitals of his ship, Captain Grant had improvised a lead barricade at the top of the balcony. He had removed sections of inner wall from his master's cabin and lined them irregularly along the top railing, in case Ilmar took a notion to try to get up there. Ilmar couldn't see him, but he could see the blaster's barrel poking through a small hole at the very center of the stairs' summit.

"Bully for you, Captain!" Ilmar rasped out. "I've got something to tell you. I—"

"Don't say anything, Jonah. Don't say you're sorry McGinn and Brooks are dead or I'll cut you to hell!"

"I know how you must feel."

"Do you? *Do you?* You—" The epithets he employed were choice gleanings of his three decades in the Fleet and they reached far back into Ilmar's ancestry. "You Jonah bastard! God, you don't know how bad I want to kill you! That scar on your slimy face is the tip-off. You're a horror-weapon some supernatural race of witches dreamed up to destroy Terra. I don't give a damn what Brooks said—Goddamn it, I—"

Ilmar moved fast, missing the first death-spit down at him. He crouched behind the ladder, too near the forewall for Grant to be able to see him without revealing himself more than he dared. He choked down a groan. Captain Grant raved on in sobbed-out hysteria. All these weeks he had worked to get his ship back home while down in the bowels of it was this horror—gnawing away, killing Brooks, killing the ship. . . .

"When you're out in space as much as I've been," Grant shout-babbled, "you have plenty of time to read. I like to read Terran history. Ancient history. Did you ever hear of Finns, Jonah? The Finns were an ancient north country race. Supposed to be wizards. They controlled the natural elements. They had power to change things. Terran sailors wouldn't let a Finn on board because he could sing up a storm and kill them all. He could send

29

one of those old sailing ships onto an iceberg anytime he wanted to. That's you, Jonah! Only now it's the great wide ocean of space. You're a Jonah, Ilmar. *You're a Finn-jonah!*"

It came like heat lightning. It hurt his brain, the sudden piercing thrust of urgent knowledge. For one fraction of time he knew everything!

"Captain!" he yelled out. "I know! I know now!" He moved out of hiding eagerly. "Listen to me, while it's still there! *I know that what you said is true!*"

Captain Grant's howl was a cave-primitive's shriek at sight of some hideous demon. The flame from the barrel of his blaster was a convulsive expression of his maniac fear. For Ilmar, time stretched out like a rubber band. He saw the white streak of sunhot death lick the air as if it moved slowly, very slowly.

He wrenched back in slow motion; he had time to half-turn before he fell into the plumbless black hole.

It was curious to be alive. Knowledge was gone, plucked back again into limbo. But he was alive and aware. After the machine-things had finished prodding him and buzzing around they left him alone. A voice spoke out of the sterile white wall.

"How are you feeling, Ilmar?"

He sat up, wincing. How did he feel? While remembrance of the ship washed over his forebrain he grimaced and plucked at the wires of his red beard. How did he feel? What a question! The invisible voice seemed to understand.

"We fed you and bathed you, and you have had time to rest up a bit. What I'm asking is, are you physically up to providing the Terran Council with some information?"

"Where am I?" Ilmar countered.

The voice was gently patient with him. "In a secret place on Terra which we reserve for classified matters we wish to keep from the general public. My name is Ronsin Cairn. My field is alien psychology. The Council gave me permission to keep an eye on you, which I have done. I am glad to see that you are better."

"Thanks," Ilmar said, standing and flexing his long muscles. "What happens now?"

"We have kept you in complete isolation, as you can infer. Robots have tended to your needs and studied you as best they could. I, and your appointed medics, have observed and directed them by video."

"What about—Captain Grant? Is he—"

"Dead? Not yet. But the Council is waiting. They want to see and hear you before any decision is made. In a moment a carrier robot will fetch you down to the vid room. There you will face the High Council and make your statement. After that it will be decided what we must do with you. . . ."

Ilmar gasped when one wall of the video room dissolved; the sudden brightness burned kaleidoscopic colors on his optical nerves; after a few minutes he could see again. He was blinking out on a tiered assemblage of humans, each wearing white tunics like togas, each wearing also an august aura of knowledge and dignified impersonal omniscience.

They stared at him, frankly curious to see this monster who carried destruction within his cells. Ilmar gulped; he moved a set of fingers to touch the flaming scar on his cheek. It burned. Somehow he wanted to hide it from them. It was a demon's brand. It would disfavor their decision. Reveal . . .

The Chairman was old, with a somber beagle's face and an attitude of impatient displeasure with his task.

All of them appeared anxious to sift out truth from a universeful of enigmas. Ilmar wondered which one of them was Psychologist Cairn.

The Chairman buzzed for silence and pointed. Across from Ilmar, he now noticed, was a second video transreceiver, like his. It glowed for a moment, dazzling Ilmar's eyes; then he saw Captain Grant. The sight of his waxy, haggard face and those blades of eyes tore his nerve ends.

Captain Grant stood up, although Ilmar saw that it cost him great effort to stay on his feet. He was still military, trim, and he wore his best uniform with all the gold ribbons on it. His face was bone-thin although the eyes leaped with resolve. He had fought death to a stalemate; he was still fighting. When he flashed one quick look at Ilmar, Ilmar read the accusation in his eyes like a reflection from the guilt in his own soul.

"Captain Grant, we have some of your statements on tape. Thank you for seeing us in person. We wish to confirm—"

"My ship!" Grant rasped. "What about my ship!"

The Chairman's dewlaps quivered when he shook his gray head. "Sorry, Captain Grant. Your ship had to be destroyed while it was still in lunar isolation. Our radars detected the erractic nature of your approach out of time-skip soon enough to become alarmed, especially when you didn't answer our signal. The ships sent out to accompany you to Luna Port were horrified to see a twisted, pitted mass of metal that could barely make it out of the time-fog. By the use of shields and laser net they managed to tug you to Luna. After you and the subject-defendant had been removed, by robot, everything involved in the misadventure was carefully destroyed."

Grant's half-mad eyes wrenched from the Chairman to

Ilmar. For a moment it looked as if sanity was completely gone again. Love for his ship did that. A sparse figure with a wisp of white hair left, stood up. The beagle-Chairman listened to him for a moment, nodded. Ilmar watched the paperthin figure, addressed as Scientist Cairn, walk closer to the video image of Captain Grant. There was a long moment of unheard conversation between them, after which Scientist Cairn turned to the Council.

"What specific information do you require? Please be brief."

"Mostly we want to be sure that Captain Grant's ship did not brush the destructive fringe of the nebular Storm area. We must be very certain that—"

Grant blazed out.

"I am responsible for all that happened! I take full blame! I allowed my two crew members to influence me, play on my sympathies about the derelict! But I did not touch the fringe area of the Storm! I swear it!"

"Then we must assume the incredible," the Chairman sighed. "The derelict did cause the disaster. And he himself is immune!"

Ilmar watched Grant's hand flail out and point at him; the sharp eyes blazed out like a maniac's. "Look at him! Sure he is immune! He's a space-jonah!"

"Jonah?"

"I know scientists laugh at space legends, just as they did centuries back on Terra itself. But you—all of you— you go out there. Listen to the alien winds howl through that black nothing for thirty years. After a while you'll find yourselves wondering just what is real and what isn't, the way I did. . . ." He choked off, bent almost double in retching physical pain, then his voice lashed out again. "They're superhumanly clever—Jonahs! The old sailors on Terran oceans knew. Those Finns could call up storms, destroy the ships. They knew *they* couldn't die. See that brand on his face? See? They've all got a mark, a red mark, on them. He's got it. He was put on that rock to destroy—to destroy—"

The slim uniformed figure shook like a willow; the muscles sheathing his bones fought to hold on; pain writhed his face. Then he fell and after a while there was only the black uniform and the ribbons.

Ilmar was immune to horror by now, as he was immune to the Black Storm. He looked into the video window with an appearance of indifference. Could a man live under the weight of all this guilt? he wondered numbly. Was he an unnatural alien monster planted on that rock to kill Terra, the central core of the human race?

Something very like a sigh of relief shivered over the assemblage when Captain Grant fell and the video light went dark. Ilmar understood. The "misadventure," as Chairman Moore termed it, was a closely guarded secret; this triple-ring of men bore the brunt of a prodigious burden. Alive, Captain Grant was capable of spreading the Storm's contagion, as much as Ilmar was. Now he was dead. Everything concerning the "misadventure" was destroyed. Everything except Ilmar.

Scientist Cairn's voice was curt and caustic.

"Ilmar, who are you?"

Ilmar stared at them all, his caved face pale as ashes under the jaunty fringe. He looked calm enough, but the storm raging in his skull belied the placidity.

"I don't know."

"Are you an alien?"

"No, I am not an alien."

Chairman Moore's voice shredded the audio. "Of course

you're an alien. We've checked all the records. Terra and all of the colonies. Nobody claims you."

"He speaks space-idiom. His test reactions indicated human intelligence."

"Then let him tell us who he is and why he alone is immune."

Ilmar was space-cold, then sun-hot. "Damn you, I keep telling you I can't remember!"

"Can you think of any reason why we shouldn't rid ourselves of you without further delay?"

Cairn said, "I can."

"Well?"

"We've been superlatively careful with him. Only robotics have been allowed close to him and they, in turn, are kept in isolation after washing. The public is unaware of his existence, to prevent panic. We all know that the nebular menace called the Black Storm is snowballing and moving our way. We have never run across anything, human or alien, that was able to resist it so far. This man is unique. We must find out *why!*"

The nods were grudging and slow to come. Cairn turned back to Ilmar. "Captain Grant made reference to an ancient ethnic group, the Finns—one of the North European cultures. Like all of the others, the Finns have long since been assimilated into our total Terran culture, and rightly so. Grant spoke about the legend of the 'jonah.' I believe the concept originated in the old Judeo-Christian mythos, garbled out of a legend about a man swallowed by a 'great fish' and living inside of it. I've heard mention of the 'jonah' myth in Space, one among many many others." He shrugged. "Be that as it may, listen carefully, Ilmar. Does any of this—"

Chairman Moore swept him aside.

"We haven't time for superstition, Cairn. It's easy to see where the reference came from—Captain Grant's traumatic experience, all those horrible weeks alone at the controls of his doomed ship. Not to mention mental deterioration of an organic nature."

"One moment!" Cairn pleaded. "Something Grant babbled on his early tapes—"

"No. Sorry."

The membership agreed with Moore. There was no time for goblins and gremlins. They had a decision to make; it must not be prolonged. Moore signaled to unseen attendants and Ilmar's view of the council chamber vanished.

He sank down on a metal bench with a convulsive shudder. He longed for the comfort of madness. He didn't care what happened to him any more. Kill him! Get done with it!

When the light came on again, he rose stiffly and faced them. Chairman Moore consulted the triple row of red-and-green lights in front of him, as if to make assurance doubly sure. The lights corresponded to the council seats; they had all voted and all of the lights except one were red. Cairn had resumed his seat and Ilmar caught a flash of stormy sympathy in his look.

Moore stood up with official dignity.

"Our decision has not been easy but we dare not wait. We have no recourse but to abide by our own precedence. Alien Ilmar: you will be removed to your isolation cubicle, and tomorrow morning you will be placed in a rocketship under automatic control. The ship will be set on an unalterable trajectory for our sun. Since there is grave question that our usual methods of destructing undesirables would not work in your case, we are taking this unprecedented way of burning away the contamination within your cells, forever."

## V

ILMAR wailed when he first saw open sky. It lashed his his soul with a kind of acrophobic terror and the hideous memory of spacial horrors, after weeks entombed. It was the darkest hour, the one just before a bleak autumnal dawn. Thunder clouds bagged the far-off lonely horizons and gray-purple rain-rags scudded overhead like fleeing ghosts.

When the carrier robot opened and told him to get out, he clawed the box walls, fighting his panic.

Outside of the carrier box was a wide black-topped field, a perfectly ordinary solar flight field but on some rock-island far away from the Cities. And this field was manned entirely by robots. Looming some hundred yards from the wheeled robot that had brought him here was the ship.

It was small: a small black spear pointing up into the cloud-fraught dark. It didn't have to be big to accommodate just him. And no use wasting materials. This was going to be a one-way trip.

After a third prodding by the controlled robot, he stepped down. The sky saw him and spoke with stentorian thunder.

"Ukko!" he called up.

Again the sonorous rolling of thunder. Lighting gashed the distant hills. Infinite power told his cellular being: *I am here, Ilmar. I am with you.*

The macrocosmic-microcosmic voice of power brought him strength. Striding briskly toward the ladder and the gaping oval hatchway, Ilmar smiled.

Robot guards moved along with him, at a distance. Walking the matte black wetness with a kind of swagger, Ilmar became aware of ships buzzing and hovering over the field in cautious circles. These would be manned. These would be taking careful account of his death-march and the ship's takeoff, so that the Council would know that its decision had been carried out and the alien menace was gone forever.

Ukko's thunder vibrated through the smallest parts of his cells and told him that what was about to happen was not of the least importance. At the top of the oval hatch was a green light winking on and off. When Ilmar had climbed up that brief ladder and through that hatch, it would go out; the ship would know it was time to leave, and when one of the controlled robots pushed a button, off it would go on its rendezvous with Sol and eternity.

He quickened his stride.

*"Ilmar!"*

The voice came from behind, to his left. It was a feminine voice, sharply urgent, and it came mingled together with a faint chopping whirr as of wings. He turned. Nothing. He shrugged and moved on. One stride only.

"Ilmar! Come to me! *Hurry!"*

He stopped. He couldn't move either way. The girl's voice was a shrill sob, both begging and demanding. It came from the center of the wingbeat sound, invisibly; now it burst out in a strange language of lapping vowels and reiterative consonants like pounding storm tides. And Ilmar understood it! He knew it! Her rush of beseeching idiom washed up on the locked doors of his memory and whispered fragrant tales of lost dreams.

All of this burst out of nothing. Invisibility.

Ilmar stared hard. Now it did seem as if the wisps of morning fog were being disturbed by unseen wings.

"Ilmar! *Kuula hyvä! Alkoon oltako kuolletu! Ole tarpeellinen!"*

"*Parempi kuelle*," he said.

"Ilmar, *rakas!* No!"

"Who are you?" he demanded harshly.

"Aino! Don't you know me? You've got to, Ilmar. We are here to save you!"

"We?"

"Nyyrikki and me!"

"Nyyrikki?"

"Your best friend, your comrade from boyhood. Don't you remember us? What have they done to you!"

"It happened before, at the lip of the Storm."

"Now I understand. *She* did it! But we must hurry—the ships will begin to wonder. Come—get in!"

Ilmar couldn't move. He strained his eyes in the direction of the voice and now it did seem as if the drifting mist encased something, a craft, an invisible ship with a copter's mobility.

A new voice broke in, a rich ringing voice that bubbled with vitality. "Hey, Sword-Face! Get over here so we can get you back where you belong."

"Nyyrikki?" The name came familiarly to his lips. The ringing laughter behind it, the insistence that life was a picnic and to hell with being serious about anything, all of this charged through him, battering at the locked doors.

"Who else would risk his neck for you, Copper-chin? Now, get those lanky legs moving! Look! The robots are getting restive—see? They're starting to close in. We may be invisible to them but we don't deflect blast. One random hit and we've had it!"

"Please, Ilmar," the girl pleaded. "The whole island's alive with war-robots. This is one of the Fleet bases. I'm tuned in to the robot-controls; they're alerting the whole robot army toward us . . ."

Hope washed him like a joyful tide. He hadn't dared to

hope for life. Continuance as a separate organism was too much to ask. No. It was the knowing that he was not alone in the universe, that at least two others cared enough for him to risk their lives. His mind rocked under the wonder of it.

He made three steps toward the swirling nothing, stopped, frozen.

"No! I can't! Don't you see—Aino, Nyyrikki? I'm walking death!"

"Not for us!" Aino wailed.

"How do you know I'm not? I must have been inside the Black Storm. I'm deadly. Get away—before it's too late!" He whirled, gnawing his tight lips. He moved toward the ship's ladder. When the voices came again, he ignored them.

He was reaching for the first rung when a round hand spun him. He got a tumbling glimpse of a grinned square-jaw face and a shock of black curled hair before the fist attached to the stocky figure contacted his copperclad chin, hard.

"Nyyrikki! No!"

A second fist rapped him, buckling his knees. There was a friendly matter-of-factness to the whole procedure. He had no time to react. The world careened and there he was being hauled away from the ship and dumped into the seat of a vessel he still couldn't see.

"Get going, Aino!" the laughing voice prompted.

"Nyyrikki—"

"Get! Take him to Kaleva. The Vanhat need him, not me. *Menne!*"

The whirled-away voice and an indignant protest boiling up within him sloughed off some of the effects of the two cracks on the jaw. Ilmar lifted, squinting, blinking into the suddenly dawn-goldened mist. A dark figure was loping swiftly to the death ship's ladder and up. Nyyrikki was whistling a woodbird trill and next to him in counterpoint Aino was crying. From all sides the war-robots were hemming in the invisible ship; sight of that tunicked figure moving up the ladder and entering the doom rocket halted them. From the sky came the whine of the manned overseer vessels.

Ilmar made a grab for the girl's arm as she moved her hands across the controls. She was still weeping. The sudden rise of new dawn over the ocean burst with roaring flame as the black rocketship quivered in its own heat and moved sunward.

In the diversive rage of Nyyrikki's purloined takeoff, the invisible ship lifted, too. As they moved above the clouds, cutting the circle of watching Fleet vessels, Ilmar caught a first good look at Aino. The girl in the control seat by his side had large violet eyes and an oval face framed by waves of chestnut-brown hair; her lips were the color of dewy cranberries. Her slim well-curved figure was sheathed in a silver-gray tunic. Aino was beautiful, even in her passion of grief for Nyyrikki.

"He promised me," she choked out.

"Nyyrikki was always good at promises." Ilmar wrenched the perception out of agony. "He knew that would stop the robots long enough for us to get away. All they knew was that there had to be somebody on that ship, and who else would want it?"

Aino nodded mistily as the craft reached a stratospheric altitude and leveled off. Ilmar gripped the arms of his foam-padded couch-seat tight, to believe that this was really happening, while he stared at her in awe. The aroma of her brown hair, the warmth of her closeness, the love in her eyes; all of this thickened his throat and slammed his heart against his ribcage in a wild bolero.

"We must now do Nyyrikki the honor of accepting his sacrifice as it was meant." Her hand touched his.

Ilmar pulled away sharply.

"What is it, *rakas?*"

"You touched me. Don't you know I'm lethal?"

"Not to me." Her cranberry lips lifted slightly. "Not to any of the Vanhat. As a matter of fact, I don't believe you did any of those terrible things. Not your body, at least. Your spacesuit, perhaps. Or maybe Captain Grant's ship picked up the contagion somewhere else in the Storm area."

Ilmar frowned, puzzled.

"How do you know all of this? You didn't know about my memory loss."

"The Vanhat have spies among the Ussi. You and I were among them in disguise often, don't you—oh, I forget! You don't remember. Never mind. We've got a long trip ahead of us. Rest."

Ilmar sighed. His long body sank gratefully on the contoured length of the twin control seat. If he could manage to forget Nyyrikki and those deaths on the ship, maybe he could really sleep for the first time in months.

"How come they don't put a trace on us?" he asked, over a yawn.

"The main Fleet bases are all on Luna and Mars. These island bases are small potatoes, by comparison. And since the war action mostly takes place in Deep Space the Terran counteractivity is a little rusty. Anyway, our Vanhat witchcraft scrambles their fixes as fast as they make them, just as it makes our ships invisible."

Ilmar looked out at the smudged lights of other ships moving sluggishly into their morning's tasks, none of these seemed aware of the Vanhat craft darting among them. He thought about what Captain Grant had said. Wizards and demons who controlled the elements. . . .

"Witchcraft?"

"The Vanhat have always been experts at creating tangible illusion. This is part of our genetic heritage from Otava. That is why we have survived, aloof and hidden from the Ussi, all these centuries."

"Ussi?"

"The New Breed. All of Terra besides the Vanhat."

Ilmar frowned in thought. "This witchcraft makes us superior to the Ussi?"

"Not superior. Different. In a way vulnerable and responsible." She flashed him a fast smile. "Why don't you sleep?"

"Can't. Now I want to know everything there is to know."

Aino sighed. "Better wait for Kaleva. It's a long, complex affair and I doubt if I can tell it right. Might be best to let it come gradually." She flicked a button on the panel. "Reach out that flask and have a shot or two. It's like brandy, but with a mild sedative. Help you to rest. You'll need it."

Ilmar swigged from the plastic container. It was wine-heady, delicious, but it did nothing for his suddenly alert and anxious forebrain.

"Seems funny," Aino said.

*"Funny?"*

"Strange. That the Son of Ilmarinen doesn't know the old songs. The whole history of the Suomi."

Ilmar took another, deeper pull at the brandy. "It's not funny to me. Can't you fill me in just a little?" He grinned while he coaxed, "Maybe then I can sleep, *rakas*."

Aino nodded gravely. "Okay. A touch of ancient history, perhaps. On one of the Scandinavian peninsulas, many centuries ago, was a country called Suomi. Finland, because of its lakes and marshes. Long before any form of written history made its appearance on the earth, a primitive-seeming people made their villages and nightfires on the edges of Suomi's rocky shores and by the blue lakes. They kept strangely to themselves, even from their nearest neighbors. They kept their odd language pure and inviolable—as they always have. Around the night-fires the finest singers would chant song-stories of Otava and of the three great heroes. While the cavemen of Iberia were painting animal pictures on the walls of Altamira and the skin-clad islanders to the north were building Stonehenge, this strange race of wizards tilled their lands, fished, hunted in the deep forests, and sang their songs.

"Their songs held fragmentary knowledge of the world in the Great Bear—"

"*Ursae Majoris,*" Ilmar blurted. "Why did they leave Otava?"

Aino's eyes clouded. "I don't know. But I *think* it was because the rest of their race evolved out of their physical bodies and became part of the universe itself. Our group either wished to keep their physical substance— or were not ready for the great change. . . ."

"A tag-end backward group?"

"Perhaps." Aino shrugged off the surge of impenetrable thoughts. "Let's get back to the Vanhat. The remnants of mind-magic they carried with them in their genes could cause things to *become*—it could under certain conditions take command of the elements, soothe storms or—"

"Or cause them!" Ilmar thought grimly of Captain Grant's dying outburst. Grant had been right!

"No," Aino said. "I know all about the old sailor tales. Finns were Jonahs because a Finn could stick his *pukko* in the ship's mast and extract a tot of rum out of it any time he wanted one. . . . That he could call up a storm. . . . Don't you see? I don't know about the rum, but he *could* sense a storm coming so accurately that they said he caused it. It was simple precognition—well, not so simple in the case of the Vanhat. *It comes from our own.*

All of our magic comes from the existence of our evolved race expanded throughout the stars!"

Ilmar jumped up and yelled:

"Then, with their help, we can do anything!"

"Certainly not," Aino laughed. "If that part of the legend is true and our evolved Otavan offshoot does exist in us and around us and throughout the universe, they are not interested in such trivial matters as tots of rum or even atomic explosions. They are beyond all that.

"There is another aspect to our so-called magic. Sometimes we call it Ukko, because Ukko is our Power God of the thunder and lightning. What it involves is what the Ussi do in their chemical laboratories. A breakdown of things into component parts. A manipulation mentally of all chemical spectra—"

"Changing the vibration pattern?"

"Yes. Kaleva makes it sound simple. Some of the Vanhat still possess the Power and know how to use it; others have it in their genetic chromosomes, but not the key . . ."

"Kaleva is our leader?"

"A true Son of Vainomoinen, the greatest wizard of all. As you are true Son of Ilmarinen. But Kaleva is old, old, old. He will not be with us long; so it is up to you, Ilmar . . ."

But the nostrum in the brandy had taken hold. Ilmar's copperclad face was cradled in the crook of his arm. He slept the sleep of a child, a child who has stumbled wretchedly through the benighted depths of a black forest and has suddenly had the night curtain pulled aside to reveal a shining garden of incredible wonder. . . .

The invisible ship hurtled onward, now down toward a god's frown of snow-shagged cliff. And right into it!

Ilmar woke up in time to yell out.

Aino smiled.

## PART TWO

## UNDEREARTH

"Thereupon smith Ilmarinen,
He the great primeval craftsman,
Welded it and hammered at it,
Heaped his rapid blows upon it—
Forged with cunning art the Sampo."

KALEVALA: *Runo X*

# VI

THE DEATH Ilmar braced himself for, the driving bash against that misted cliff, didn't come. Instead—a blur on the retina, a puff of cloud on a brassy September's daybreak. Like the ship's invisibility reversed by Otavan magic—the jutting crag and death itself was illusion. . . .

What Ilmar saw as the ship glided to a slow landing tangled up in his throat and pained him with beauty. He saw a salmon-gold sunrise weave a carpet of colors across the dark shadows of lofty mountains. He saw the effulgence of it dance with light steps into a wide valley of lake and spruce forest. A village of small log houses couched by twinkling birches and that deep velvet lake. He gulped, blinked stinging eyes, while the dawn changed the first season snow on the rooftops from blue-white to rose-white. Blue woodsmoke from the sod chimneys lazed up; now a gentle morning breeze sent long silver shivers across the velvet lake. Far above the valley, Otava's dipper of stars winked out, one after one.

"Ilmar!"

The old man's arms embraced him while deposed grief shuddered up in gurgles from within that long, white, patriarchal beard.

Ilmar's mind struggled with the sealed doors, aided and abetted by the poignant swords of memory. Seeing all of this. Seeing this tall ancient in his homespun wool robe. The snowy beard and the crinkled eyes behind round thin-rimmed glasses tinted bright blue. The old gnarled hands wore brown pigment spots from the crush of time, and now they helped his old, old eyes to see Ilmar, trembling up from his shoulders to the red scar on his cheek.

"Don't you know me, my son?"

"Kaleva?" Ilmar wasn't sure whether he really remembered yet, or that Aino had mentioned the ancient Vanhat leader's name. "We call you that because you are our oldest and greatest hero. Because we love you!" It flooded out. "Because you teach us the old songs of Otava."

The old man nodded. When he spoke, in the old tongue which the Vanhat alone had kept, it was like quavery singing. He chuckled in his beard. "Do not be afraid, Ilmar, my son. You will remember all that you must, in due course. Here in your true home with all of your friends. With Aino." He pointed at the path to the Greathouse, at the center of the village. Already the new snow had been packed down by many booted feet, and there they all were—as many as could—lined ten deep along the rising path. They wore colorful woolens, the kind their ancestors of ancient times had worn, for this joyful occasion; their glad shouts to Ilmar and chatter among themselves sent little puffs of condensation mist across the brisk autumn dawn.

"See how glad they are that you have returned to us, Ilmar?" His arm held Ilmar on one side, Aino on the other, while they moved between the Vanhat, who shouted greetings and tried to touch the star wanderer returned to his people.

"Where are we going?" Ilmar asked Aino.

"Can't you guess?" Kaleva chuckled. "The women have prepared a feast. It will be in the manner of the ancients, here in the Greathouse and—"

"Excuse me, Father," Aino said, when they stepped

through the open double-doors onto the plank floor. "Look! Someone else has come to greet Ilmar!"

Ilmar turned. He swept his look into the blaze of sunrise, squinting, then shading his eyes. Down the path out of the wood a small dark figure was hurrying. He watched, still not understanding the welling lump in his throat and his hammering heart. The tall figure with the blue shawl over her graying hair moved down through the scarlet-toqued villagers and the yapping dogs in a whirl of excitement. She stopped, waved at him, came on.

On the first step she stopped to tap the snow off her high old-fashioned shoes, wipe furtively at her eyes with a corner of her kerchief. She moved up, faced him. Her face was lined and bony, her shoulders were round and gawky under her shawl; her plain peasant's dress had a blue apron over it. While she peered at Ilmar with old anxious eyes, fearful of seeing changes and hurts in him, her shawl fell back to show straight bunned hair with streaks of white penciled through it. The drinking eyes were fiercely blue with flecks of argent silver in them.

"You are home, Ilmar."

"Yes." He might have returned from an early hunt for grouse in the forest. But something had hold of his entire being, physical, mental, and whatever else the children of Otava were. She could not move either, at first. Their eyes and their souls touched.

Then he said it and this time no locked door could hold it back, nor any midwife's sharp knife. "*Aiti.*"

Lokka said nothing. She was in his arms with a great glad cry; Ilmar rocked with her, back and forth, back and forth.

The long table of the Greathouse groaned with the feast the women had been hoarding for his homecoming. Ilmar gnawed fresh salmon and bear-steak with relish; he downed a huge mug of *kallia;* he stuffed his lean, hunger-gaunt body with milk-bread and sweetened cranberries from the bog. Never had it been so fine to be alive, nor so important to stay that way. The warmth of all his friends' smiles, the nearness of Lokka on one side and Aino on the other—and Kaleva telling Jumala of their great joy in the hero's safe return—all of this coalesced to produce within his veins a kind of mad delirium. Especially considering the all-consuming despair that had seemed his lot such a short time ago. Such happiness was too much to believe or to bear. Nor could such happiness last.

The Vanhat at the feast allowed themselves no such qualms. Young Vaino played on his *kantele* and sang with lively passion. The laurel-hung rafters of the Great-hall rang with songs, so that the *bessalintut* from Tapio's green forest came to the open-flung sills of the hall to listen in envy.

Sang young Vaino:

> *"O thou wondersmith, Ilmarinen,*
> *Wherefore is thy mind so saddened?*
> *Said the smith, e'en Ilmarinen,*
> *'Yes, my thoughts are home directed*
> *To my land, that I may live there,*
> *Rest among those scenes familiar . . .'"*

Ilmar's heart could not contain his joy. Every face was somehow familiar, every handclasp held ringing truth—even the pungent aroma of the wood in the kitchen stove and the smell of the warm fresh bread—all of this was *his.* His for now. His to savor and believe and love. What could the great Cities offer that could compare? What could the stars themselves offer?

Seeing that his beer mug was empty, understanding

the quixotic torment of his rediscovered happiness, Lokka ladled him out another great horn of the dark brew.

Ilmar offered some to Aino. She smiled and sipped. Then he dipped into the foam with a wide grin.

Vaino sang:

> *"Stainless sits the maid beside thee,*
> *Maiden bright to thee affianced,*
> *Pledged to thee in all her beauty."*

Ilmar set down his mug and turned to Aino. But the girl had left her seat. From the doorway she looked back, her eyes storming with tears.

"What did I do?" Ilmar asked Lokka.

"Nothing, my son. It was the song. You see, the wedding Vaino sang about was yours—but not hers."

"Who else?" Ilmar demanded.

"Not now." Her hand touched his. "Kaleva wishes that you enjoy all the good olden things now. That you are happy. Let the trouble come later. The secret sorrow is always with us." He felt her shiver as she grasped his hand.

"What secret—?"

"I'm sorry, Ilmar. It just came out of me. Please don't ask yet. Kaleva will tell you all—and all too soon." Her voice dwindled to a whispered sigh.

Ilmar scowled down at his half-empty mug. Joy was indeed fleeting. The laughter, the songs, held an undertone of desperation in them. The Vanhat were holding back some great dam of fear. . . .

Hero. They called him hero. Yet Ilmar knew he was not. He had tried to be a hero. That was what had taken him out of their secret illusion-protected valley, a valley that dreamed lost dreams but was really a sham itself. The log huts. The homespun dress. The feast of fish from the lake and forest animals. All of this was of itself illusion. It had no place in Earth I, with its complex technology and star-flung economy.

Why?

What was their terrible secret?

Why must these ancestors of the ancient wizards and warlocks hide themselves from the rest of the world?

He had the sudden bitter feeling that he did not want to be here. He did not want to belong to the Vanhat. He belonged out there—with Cairn and the Ussi.

Then, in a well-polished compote of sugared strawberries, he saw his face. Distorted, twisted by the curving surface, with the crimson sword blazing double-size across his cheek.

His hands made fists, his teeth pressed his lips and jaw into a tight line. *I belong*, he muttered silently. *I belong*.

The sound of a great bell, sharp and incisive, cut through his self-searching. It was somber, deep-toned, and it demanded immediate attention of all at the feast.

This it got. The songs were instantly hushed. Even the children stopped their laughing chatter, as if conditioned to it like Pavlov's dogs.

"What is it?" Ilmar's demand cut the silence like a knife.

Nobody answered him. At the other end of the long table Kaleva rose with majestic dignity, but his face was suddenly eon-old and very sad. He smiled down the table, but the smile was haunted.

"Vanhat, it is time. We must go to Underearth. We have had our Day."

## VII

UNDEREARTH. The very sound of it was like a tomb's door closing. Is that what it was, really? Were the Vanhat really only ghosts who must descend to their graves after their one day of each year among the living? Were they accursed, by some eldritch magic of their own making? Ilmar wondered suddenly if the ship had slammed against the cliff and if he, like the rest of them, was dead and buried.

Was this the true illusion? Was the village, the shimmering lake, the feast, the songs—were all these things only the *illusion* of life?

When Lokka beckoned him, he followed her like an obedient boy. But following, rebellion began boiling up inside of him. He would not be dead! He would not go to Underearth! He was alive—all of him! Never had his muscles and his nerves felt more alive than right now. Let them go back to their graves, not Ilmar!

Kaleva led the solemn procession at a lagging pace out of the Greathall, down the smoke-scented path where the sun was already melting the winter's first snow blanket. Mothers kept a firm grip on childish hands so that they wouldn't run back to play in the bright patches. Old *muumus* with bent backs and gnarled canes hobbled to keep up. As Kaleva's tall form reached the woods, Ilmar blinked from the sun-sheen dripping melted beads off the soughing pine branches.

A winding path brought the silent cortege to the foot of a great cliff facing north. This broken escarpment leaped into driving mists and it was here that Kaleva halted them. His blue tinted glasses reflected the morning sun when he turned, as if to devour a long last look at the valley of the Vanhat. Then he nodded to his flock and vanished into a narrow cave-arch. Ilmar saw that there were old logs shoring up the cave; it had the look of a mine shaft, unused since the ancients.

He lingered, watching them file in. Two tassel-hatted twins went into a tantrum and their father had to grab them, one under each arm, and carry them, kicking, into the dark.

Lokka turned. "Come, Ilmar. It is time."

The haunted resignation in her face struck fire in Ilmar's brain. "No! I won't go in that black hole!"

He whirled and ran. Lokka called after him urgently; others stopped and called, too. But the mugs of beer and his taste of freedom and happiness burned in him like a raging fire. It was his nature to lead, to rebel. His star-trek had been both. He had left the Vanhat before in some wild youthful rage of pent-up concupiscence that demanded action, even though Kaleva said it was not time yet. *The Gate is not open!* Kaleva had admonished him. *Wait! You must have the Sword!* But Ilmar had not waited, and the results of his folly brought disaster. Now they were dragging him back to more waiting. . . .

He ran with these thoughts washing over him, unheeding both the implicit warning they brought and the mind-calls of the Vanhat. *Come back! You will die!*

He reached the shadowed range of high mountains to the South. That was where he would go. South, to the great Cities. Whirling about, he spotted what looked like a narrow ravine, a pass through. He was in fog now, sifting, clinging fog. He plunged further in toward the crack in the rock. Suddenly his legs wouldn't run, his arms moved in slow-motion. In a panic he found he could scarcely breathe; he fought with his fists against the rubbery web that had him trapped. One slow-motion step further in. Another. Then he screamed and fell—very, very slowly.

He dreamed.

The runners of his sledge sought out a tenuous path along the birch-lined lake. The rowan cumber rattled as the chestnut horse strained his young muscles in the yoke to Ilmar's whip. Ilmar shouted into the stinging north wind, cracking the whip expertly over Ahava's head.

Ilmarinen the Wondersmith was still peeved. He grimaced at the neat way his wizard friend Vainomoinen had tricked him. He swore at Ahava about it, then chuckled and jammed the bead-embroidered whip back in its sheath.

"The old graybeard is a wily fox!" he told Ahava. "He is old, yet he still has his lusts, and he hopes that I—Ilmarinen, the Wondersmith—will pick his berries out of the sucking marsh! *Ai*. Old Louhi, the Witch of Pohyola, got her daughter, the rainbow siren, to ensnare even such an old graybeard as Vaino! Think of that, Ahava. With all his years. True, his voice is still mellifluous to charm the birds out of Tapio's trees and the crows into drowning themselves out of envy—but he is ancient and the juices have run dry. So Louhi tells him that he may marry her entrancing daughter on one condition." Ilmar laughed into the howling wind. "What do you think that condition is, my fast one! It is that he must build for Witch Louhi the magic Sampo. *The Sampo!* The Star Mill that will grind out anything one may ask of it. The wonder-machine that will snatch god-power from beyond the stars and create things out of the smallest particles of air and sea and rock. What manner of things? Anything! Anything that exists anywhere in the stars!"

Ilmar pulled the left rein fast and swore at Ahava to

miss the looming knoll of bare rock like a demon's head with blue-gray snow for hair. The right runner screamed over bare rock, the sledge tilted perilously, then righted. With a toss of mane and a show of teeth, Ahava pushed wind and on.

The wind was chill, and getting more so. Ilmar took time to brush the upswept snow off his red beard and shaggy eyebrows, then confided the rest of his ignominy to Ahava since there was no one else on the bleak journey to listen.

"So, naturally, old Vaino came to *me*. Me—Ilmarinen, the greatest smith of all. *Kyllä*. Was it not I who forged the sky above us? Were not the stars sparks out of my blazing forge when I accomplished this feat? Was it not I who melted raw gold to fashion the moon and to—"

Ahava gave a loud back-snort for such bragging. Ilmarinen grumbled at the sudden noise, gave him a remonstrative taste of whip, then went on.

"I must confess that Vainomoinen, my oldest friend, used a clever trick to put me on my way to Pohyola. Getting me to climb up that great pine to fetch the moon down for him to prove that I had indeed made it—then sang up such a storm that it caught that pine tree up, roots and all, and hurtled me off into space in the direction of the Witch's gloomy island in the sky."

Ahava's shrugged back-glance seemed to ask: "Then why did you not go back after this ship-tree spilled you back down on the shores of this gloom-haunted place? Why did you sing up this sledge and steal me out of my warm barn, to continue your journey across this tundra to Pohyola's Castle?"

"*Perkele!*" was Ilmarinen's grouchy answer.

With her usual courtesy to human visitors, when Ilmarinen reached the courtyard of Louhi's black stone castle, she set the dogs on him. Ilmar heard her cackling at one of the windows while the ill-fed creatures snapped at Ahava's heels and tore bits of rawhide and wool off Ilmarinen's leggings when he got out. Ilmarinen was giving the wild-eyed monsters something to think about with his whip when Louhi, her sadistic mood sated, sent them yelping and cringing in the down-meadow direction of the swine-pens. A stablekeep took charge of Ahava and Ilmarinen tramped swearing into a side door of the castle.

He demanded food for his empty belly. A wretched slave-girl servant brought him cold barley gruel and sour beer. His language frightened the bats in the rafters as he flung the tray across the stone floor.

Louhi cackled delightedly, hiding behind a pillar; then she moved out into the small, cold chamber. Ilmarinen squinted at her from under his coppery bushes. The black shawl and the ragged apron which she affected did not fool him. Her ugly dark face with the eyes glinting malevolently out of deep sockets told him at once who she was and what.

"What is this *sonta*—for Suomi's greatest hero!"

Louhi hid a toothless smile and adjusted the black shawl over her hump. Her claw held fast to the rowan snake-stick that was her badge of membership among the star-demons of the Black Nebula.

She gave him a mocking curtsey and a beggar woman's whine. "You can see from the bareness of the room, and the skinniness of my servants and my dogs, that I am very poor, and I can offer you no better."

"You lie, Witch!" Ilmarinen tramped the room in a fury. "I—Ilmarinen, the Wondersmith—have traveled all the way from Lake Imari to visit you and your daughter. And this is the treatment I receive!"

"Ah! Why did you not say so at once! My beautiful daughter shall wait upon you, herself!"

She clapped her hands. Servants appeared. Food appeared in trenchers that steamed with succulent meats and gravies and plump potatoes. Pohyola's fabulous daughter herself brought in a copper pitcher of dark ale to wash it down.

Ilmarinen stopped wolfing down food and gaped. She was indeed the most radiant creature Ilmarinen had ever seen or dreamed of seeing. Dressed in an opalescent web-thin garment that clung to her thighs and her breasts invitingly, she wore sapphires that formed an exciting pattern on the opal; and as if that were not enough, small silvery bells on her ankles and wrists, bells that tinkled when she moved toward him, smiling with red, red lips.

"One has heard of Pohyola's daughter, even to the southmost tip of Carelia," Ilmarinen gulped. "What is your name, delightful creature?"

"I have no name."

"*Niin?*"

"Speaking of names, have you on your travels heard reports of, or encountered, the great wondersmith Ilmarinen?"

"I have, child. I have met with this smith often on my journeys, for the reason that I myself am this same Ilmarinen."

The Witch's daughter gasped in awe. Louhi cackled in her throat when she saw the way Ilmarinen stared at the girl.

"He has come to forge us the Star Mill—the Sampo itself!"

"Have I?" Ilmarinen's eyes could not remove themselves from the red-mouthed girl. "What do I get for performing this marvel?"

"Why marriage with my daughter here, of course!"

So it was that next morning, before dawn fingered its cautious way through the everfogs of Pohyola, the Witch island, that Ilmarinen sought carefully for a station where he might erect his smithy and work in peace. He found a cavern halfway up a great cliff. In the center of it was a great broken thing like metal and ceramic wedded; there were colors streaking rainbowlike through this Thing, colors not seen on the earth because they had come from Otava. This, then, was the lost vessel, a magic place, and here Ilmarinen set up his bellows and his forge, together with the great black cauldrons for the melting and the dipping.

Many days and nights did the smith toil, summer nights when the sun burned somberly always through the cloud-wrack. Besides the melted Thing, he stirred in black swan plumes, the milk of a cross-eyed heifer, silver-tipped barley plucked under a gibbous moon, sheep's blood, and other magical things. And all the while he did this, Ilmarinen sang the Old Songs, song-magic dipped out from the cosmic sources of all-creation and all-power, as the Great Bear dips out stars.

Success did not come easily. Presently, staring fiercely into the iridescence bubbling in the cauldron, Ilmarinen saw a gold crossbow set with a silver arrow emerge and twang with blood-lust on the air of the shadowy cave.

"You are beautiful, my friend," the smith told it. "But you are evil."

He seized the crossbow and broke it into many pieces. These he flung back into the cauldron and told his servants to work the bellows harder than before and put more pithy-knots on the fire. Ilmarinen himself worked, out of impatience, so that sweat hissed down into the fire and yellow flames leaped up and singed his beard.

Came a boat, with silver sails, a starboat. But this, too, was of evil disposition. Ilmarinen took no pleasure in its great beauty; he smashed it without a flinch and back it went into the fire.

Now a heifer of great charm, with golden horns and

the sign of Otava on her forehead. But she, too, went
back in the pot. And a plowshare for harvesting stars.

Then, at last—

The wind snarled and howled across the ragged cliff,
like thousands of fear-crazed star demons fleeing Ukko
and his thunder. Black clouds boiled across the icy sky.
In the cave smithy, sparks leaped up out of the furnace
in a devil's dance. It was now that the Sampo arose.

First Ilmarinen saw the Star Mill's rainbow cover
forming, changing and writhing in the great cauldron. He
sang his magic louder, louder. He told the Powers behind the stars to stop building universes and build him a
Sampo. . . .

Old Louhi was well pleased. She rubbed her claws
together greedily and set about making the Sampo do its
work of grinding out things for her. Warehouses full of
things. Foods. Woolens and silks. Metals and made
things. Things to barter with her demon friends. Servants of steel. Warriors to guard her Castle. All the soar-
ing desires in her evil heart. When the storage barns her
servants built for her overflowed with things, Louhi demand that the Sampo itself build more storage houses.

While this was happening, Ilmarinen, weary to the
marrow of his bones, slept. When he finally woke and
had eaten, he went to see Louhi, sitting on a golden
throne and bedecked in silks and jewels; he stood before
her and demanded his fee.

Louhi screwed up her face at him. "Begone, smith!
Can't you see that I am busy thinking up things to *want?*"

"I want, too, Mistress. I want what I was promised."

Louhi shrugged. "Go find her for yourself, then, and
leave me in peace."

Ilmarinen found Pohjola's daughter in the meadow
behind the barns and servant quarters. Now she was no
queen in cobweb and sapphire. Now she was a sweet-

faced child in a blue peasant skirt and a modest white blouse. Her dark hair hung in brown ringlets about her milkwhite shoulders.

Ilmarinen told her she must come with him and be his bride, as was promised him by her mother.

The sweet-faced child wept:

> *"If I leave my well-loved homeland,*
> *Who shall hear the cuckoo calling,*
> *And the birds all sweetly singing?*
> *If I seek a foreign country*
> *All the cuckoos then would vanish,*
> *All the nightingales would migrate*
> *From the shores of Pohja's island.*
> *All unplucked the mountain-berries,*
> *All untrod the fragrant meadows,*
> *And the woods I love so dearly . . ."*

Such was her weeping and her poignant song that Ilmarinen stumbled away, wiping the drops of salt water off his cheeks. He sighed as he went back into the rear courtyard and bade the servants fetch his sledge and Ahava to pull it.

Cracking his beaded whip, he set his path southward to his own country, with the sound of Louhi's cackling laughter drifting down from her tower to burn his ears.

"He won't die, Father?"

"No, Aino. The stress his mind was under negated the Shield to some extent. In this way he was protected from his own rash attempt to plunge through the Illusion."

"I don't understand."

"These things are not to be understood with our minds, child. Something quivering inside of my cells tells me what is and what is not. It can't be pinned down or labeled with the mental equipment we have to work with. The Illusion surrounding our valley is strong; we purposely gave it such a concentration of reality that we ourselves are confined within it. Ilmar is special. He is of Ilmarinen himself, so his cells are close to the Power. We waited here in our self-imposed exile for many centuries for him to come; when the midwife saw the sword mark she brought him to me and I knew our long wait was near its end!"

"He stepped right into the Illusion—on this side!"

"Yes. His desire to escape was strong. His mind was confused—yet savagely strong." Kaleva sighed. "Yet, such a hero as Ilmar cannot run from destiny . . ."

Ilmar groaned and pulled himself fully awake; he blinked up at the solemn white-bearded face of Kaleva, at Aino's grave, anxious eyes brimming with fear for him.

"Where am I?"

"Easy, my son." Aino gave the cushions behind him a hike and helped his rise to a sitting position. Ilmar's brain still sang with ancestral songs; for a time he could only stare questions at the two of them.

"We brought you here to one of the infirmaries after I interrupted the Illusion and freed you," Kaleva said.

Ilmar eyed the hospital white walls, the medical cabinets, the Ussi machines for treating body ills.

"Underearth?"

Kaleva smiled gently. "We have lived down here for more than a thousand years. Ever since one of our own among the Ussi sent Hiisi and his Pahaliset back beyond the evil stars from which they came. This is your true home, Ilmar. Nor is it as bad as you have imagined. True, we are sad when our Day is over and we have to come back—sad to leave the forest and the lake. But down here we have everything we need. It has its own kind of beauty, our Underearth."

"You'll see, Ilmar!" Aino panted. "I show you everything."

Ilmar nodded. "What about the village? The log huts?"

"We keep it that way to remind us of ancient days. To tie us with Otava and the old legends. When we go up there, group by group, for our Day, we dress as the ancient Suomalinen dressed. It is a happy thing, to remember simple ways."

Aino poured Ilmar something in a glass. He drank it and felt new courage and strength pound through his veins.

"Sleep now, Ilmar. Later Aino will show you—"

He leaped off the treatment table, masking his vertigo with a brisk grin. "How about now?"

Aino took his arm and they were off.

Ilmar whistled and clicked his tongue at the ingenuity of the labyrinths which the Vanhat had carved out of the earth under their cold peninsula. They peeked into great chambers where workers were contentedly occupied at diverse tasks; everything was produced underground, all of the necessities and comforts for the community of over twenty thousand Vanhat of every age. Earth's minute scraps of mineral and chemical wealth were drained off by ingenious siphon-magnets; Ussi-type machines were employed to break down the chemical building blocks and rearrange them to the specific need. Enormous hydroponic tanks grew the Vanhat their food; Ilmar saw "gillmen" move up into the ocean above to gather in the bountiful harvest of Ahto himself.

Aino took Ilmar from one simple yet artful area of endeavor to another with shining eyes.

"They sing while they work," he said. "They're happy down here away from the sun and the stars?"

Her prideful pleasure clouded over. "Not entirely. But the singing is part of our Otava heritage."

"Yes?"

"It's the song-magic. We all have it in our bones. When the great wondersmith, Ilmarinen, created the Star Mill— when Vainomoinen the great wizard fashioned his copper sky boat—they sang. Their words and the vibratory rhythms of their believing minds *told* the thing they were creating what it must be. Their songs drew Power from behind the stars."

"I don't understand."

"Nor I. I simply believe. Kaleva says belief is the final ingredient in the formula. If you don't *believe* a thing can be, how can it—ever?"

"All these workers use this Power?"

"To a mild degree. We combine it with Ussi technology, as you see, and the results are—well, it has kept us fed and clothed and reasonably happy for a thousand years." She laughed and tugged him away from the central city of shining clean walls into great halfmoon tunnels of natural rock.

"Where now?"

"You must see our artwork. Our music chambers. And the Lake . . ."

Ilmar allowed himself to be prodded through a succession of rooms devoted to beauty. All of the arts were featured. He saw luminescent paintings of the Old Gods, imaginative wall-size fantasies of unknown Otava Valmis becoming stars and song and wind and all that exists. There were murals of Ilmatar creating the Universe, of Osmo the progenitor of Kaleva the Wise, of three-dimensional forests rich with greens and browns and Tapio himself with his animal children. There was Svojatar, the mother of all serpents. There was Kanteletar of the Rainbow, playing her golden harp. Then—

"*Who*—!"

Ilmar felt the curly copper hairs low on his neck stand up and pull flesh with them. They had come to the last of the chambers and he was vis-à-vis a hideous hag standing on a rock-crag, with the purple storm raging behind her, her maenad's hair whipped about a face of unbelievable cruelty and evil. The ancient mouth curved with pitiless craftiness; the green-fire eyes leaped out of sockets like holes in space and defied the gods themselves with such cunning and delight in pure horror that not even Ukko himself had the power to destroy it. Such essence of evil transcended time itself.

Aino's face blanched too.

"Come away, Ilmar."

He stared, transmuted by the alchemy behind these hell-green eyes into a man of stone.

"I have seen her," Ilmar ground out harshly. "I have seen the Witch of Pohyola! I have felt the rending claws of her demon hounds!"

Aino shivered against him.

"You—were—*there?*"

Memories like darting vipers leaped out of sudden cracks in the locked doors. The eternal island. The fog. The tower. The witch. His crazy inept try to find something . . . Something . . . And the baying of the huge hell's dogs as they leaped on him through the fog. And the witch's voice from the tower window. Cackling. Careless in her victory. Cackling. The sound of her horrendous cackle echoing across the great void of stars. . . .

The hag's eyes stabbed the back of his neck all the way to the misted Lake of the Black Swan.

Ilmar's vision carried him gently into the silver-blue mist that covered the far half of the lake. The roof of this wholly natural phenomenon—or as it might have been fashioned by Vipunen the Titan himself—was softly hidden by clouds that were made warm by some subterranean labyrinth of tunnels that led to icelandic volcanoes. Where he stood with Aino was a haunting-strange garden of curious lichen and ferns and orchidaceous blooms as pale as death itself. A dark rock path led to an ancient wooden pier at which was moored a black barge.

"What is out there?" Ilmar whispered. "Behind the blue mist?"

Aino shook her head. Her eyes were sad, wistfully sad. "We don't know. We must all go into the mist where the Black Swan sings. We must all, when it is time, find our rest in . . ."

"Tuonela."

Time and well-being spawned restlessness in Ilmar. He roved the patterned Underearth cities and watched the others at their tasks with envious eyes. Where was his place? He must be up and doing. He was well now. What was his task?

He told Lokka, his mother:

"Why? Why do we skulk down here like moles—away from the Ussi Cities? They send their ships flinging through the fogs of time-skip into the depths of space, and here we hide like skittish animals in the ground! Where is our future? What is the point of going on like this?"

Lokka's old eyes beseeched patience. "Kaleva has taught us the virtues of simplicity and non-violence, which the Ussi have yet to learn." She added softly, "Are they happy, in their Cities of a hundred Levels, with numbers for names?"

"No, Mother. Mostly they scramble to get on the lists that will permit them passage on a colony ship, no matter what happens to them when they get there." He smote a fist against his palm. "But, Mother! If we have these star-secrets that can help them to find happiness—isn't it our duty to do what we can? To help instead of hiding from them?"

"I think," said Lokka, with a swift nod, "that it is time for you to talk with Kaleva."

Ilmar found the old man resting his dry bones on a couch made out of carven oak, in the round mystical chamber which Kaleva reserved for deep contemplation and for vital decisions. Behind his ancient couch was a fine-spun tatter of Otavan flag, deep blue, swan white, with its curious Star Bear. There concave steps led to his couch, and a leather-cushioned three-legged stool for Ilmar to fold up his long legs and sit on, when the sage beckoned.

"I have been waiting for you."

Ilmar's copper brows hunched closer involuntarily. He could not help saying it. "Why didn't you send for me?"

Kaleva's old eyes seemed to twinkle. "There is a time for all things. Your time is now. Ask what you will."

Ilmar's mouth opened in a rush of questions, but now Kaleva's face contorted with pain and under his blue robes the centuries-ancient bones shuddered with racking coughs. Ilmar stared with pity but he knew better than to ask if he could do anything. Kaleva's drawn, pale face said it all. Time was trickling its golden grains down the glass swiftly, nearing those last shimmering flecks.

He stared around him. The walls were hung with beautiful ancient tapestries which seemed to have woven into them all the things of the earth. Grasses and reeds. Animal furs and skins. Strands of all of the metals, of copper and fine iron and the rare earth metals. Dazzling rubies and emeralds and radiant sapphires. Bits of conch shells from the bottoms of deep oceans. Pine needles and birch barks. Diamonds and swan feathers. All that exists upon the small planet which the wanderers from Otava had chosen for their new home, with anguish and love.

The four heroes were there, pictured within the lavish natural glory. There was Vainomoinen, the wizard, Vaino of the long beard and the sorcerer's robe; there was Lemminkainen, the Beautiful Warrior, young, blond, flaunting his sensuous white-toothed smile in search of new conquests in war and love; there was Kullervo, the tragic wanderer of the bleak snows; and—

Ilmar's look froze on the twenty-foot figure of a red-bearded smith bending over his forge, staring eyes-agleam from the raging yellow fire, at a shining silver sword which his sinewy muscles and his song-magic had created.

"I am ready now," Kaleva said.

Ilmar whipped his look from the copperbeard who might have been his older self.

"Why?" he blurted. *"Why?"*

Kaleva's nod was involved in a spacial sigh.

"Why are we here? Why Underearth at all? Why are we not amalgamated with the rest of Terra, absorbed into the mainstream of the planet? These are the questions you ask."

"This melting down of racial identity stopped Terran war," Ilmar said.

"And brought worse ones through overpopulation." He lifted a bony hand. "Never mind. Aino has told me about your dream or whatever it was. A kind of reliving of Ilmarinen creating the Sampo."

"You're not going to tell me he did create the Star Mill!"

"Yes. Exactly so. As you found out from Aino's historical reference, the Ussi feared us. They feared us because, even in those ancient blundering days, they sensed the potential of alien power within our people. We are of Otava and we do have access to this Power, when we know how to use it. The Ussi can use it, too, if they permit themselves to believe. We are not exclusive. The Power is there, irrefutably locked in the Source that first created the suns and the stars. We have no monopoly, but we do sometimes have the key. . . ."

"What about those of us who left the Vanhat and went into the Cities, long ago?"

"They lost the key, or perhaps it is still there, diffused among the Ussi without their knowing it. To our youth who left us, we seemed primitive. Simple. Naïve. But among 'primitives' is ESP and the other 'supernormal phenomenon' always highest. The Ussi blamed us for using what they chose to term black magic. They erred. The Vanhat have never been a belligerent people; have never started wars, only fought when provoked into it by aggressors, of which—" The old patriarch sighed and wiped his eyes behind the blue lenses. "—there have been many. Yes, our so-called primitivism sprang from the fact that our empathy with the natural elements, with all living creatures, with the metals, with everything that exists—is very strong. We sense the oneness when we look into the heart of a wood flower—or when we look up into the stars. This oneness with the universe has always been in our music, our other arts, in everything we do. Even in the middle of the Twentieth Century illiteracy was practically nonexistent with our people. If we remained aloof it was out of choice and for good reason."

Ilmar gave his head an impatient toss. "Surely there are others here on this planet who understand these things! We aren't unique!"

"No, Ilmar. We aren't. We are humans, like them, but the Otava spark within us enables some of us to *use* the mind-power linked to the source of all power which some people give the name of God. We call it Jumala. And Ukko. And Ilmatar."

"Don't tell me our people still believe in the old gods! They were all only created out of fear—they're no longer needed, as Man flings out into Deep Space—"

"Ah, my son! As Man flings out into Deep Space the gods, or whatever you choose to call these Forces, become more needful and more evident. But—forget all this. The Force *does* exist. The fact that we exist and are able to ponder about it proves it!

"Let us consider the Ussi and the progress they have made in the direction of knowledge, in spite of all their wars. Here is the pattern. First they *thought* about creating a spear or a knife to kill the animals for food. Then they created this spear or knife with their hands, out of things they found around them. This led to the atom bombs for domination, or conquest. But the *thought* was the beginning. Even when they discovered the time-glide which sent them flinging their ships out after new conquests the *thought* was father of the deed.

"So—we are *now*. The more advanced of the Ussi are beginning to ponder this thought: *why not eliminate the middle man?* Think. Build. Possess. Eliminate build. *Create the thing or power-source directly out of the mind itself.*"

Ilmar whistled.

"Which is what Ilmarinen and the Vanhat were able to do thousands of years ago, while the Ussi were blundering about with their sticks and stones to break people's bones!"

Kaleva nodded somberly.

"Yes. It has come full circle again. Then we were 'primitives' with the black magic. Now we would be hailed as pioneers, and—I very much fear, exploited."

"Now I get it." Ilmar scowled. "The Vanhat hid under

the ground to keep from revealing their star-power to the Ussi!"

"For their own good as well as ours." Kaleva nodded. "They are brilliant, their Cities are shining examples of a complex technology. Yet they aren't ready for total power. Perhaps they never will be. Perhaps it was never meant to be. The Power is dying out—even among us. Perhaps that is as it was meant to be. . . ."

Kaleva's trembling fervor sent him into a spasm of coughing again. Ilmar's blue eyes sparked with awe and an overwhelming terror. Those there were among the Ussi who would use such power to destroy, not build. First cities and countries. Then planets. Then suns. Then—

"There is no end to it!" he groaned. "Now I see why we hide. We can't unleash this—this monster!"

"Unhappily," Kaleva said with forced calm, "this monster, as you call it, has already been unleashed."

"Some Underearth renegade!"

Kaleva's eyes moved closer to Ilmar's face. "No. It is true that our people have human weaknesses, too. One among us might have done such a thing—out of fear for the Vanhat, out of hot-blood rage at having to live as we do—a hundred reasons. But we have kept our secret and taught our children Christian meekness and understanding to prevent just such a thing from happening.

"No. It happened long, long ago . . ."

"Ilmarinen, my ancestor! The Sampo!"

Kaleva sobbed a ragged breath. "Here is the rest of the legend of the Star Mill. Unfortunately it is no legend . . ."

## VIII

ILMAR's hand whipped to the flame on his face. *Now.*
Now was *time.* He must devour every word, every syl-
lable. Then, when he knew what he must know, he must
act ...

"Your ancestral dream showed you how Ilmarinen
sang the Star Mill into being. How he used broken pieces
of the ship that brought the Vanhat to earth and the
song-magic to create this terrible, beautiful thing. How
Louhi, the Witch, repented her bargain and—"

"How her daughter changed herself into a weeping
peasant child who could not bear to leave her homeland."
Ilmar snorted. "I think Ilmarinen decided then that he
didn't want a wife who could change herself any time
she pleased. Who would want such a creature—one day
a siren, the next a carping shrew ..."

"There are many different versions of what happened
after Ilmarinen left Pohyola. Around the old night-fires,
the minstrel singer of each village sings the deeds of one
of the great heroes. Naturally, through the centuries,
some of the songs are changed, little by little. There are
other versions of what happened after Ilmarinen forged
the Sampo—but this is the true one.

"The smith returned to his homeland and found his
people starving and sick. The gods of Tapiola and the
shining lakes and oceans had not been kind to them.
Ilmarinen told his old friend, the wizard, Vainomoinen:

" *'Here we starve, while in Pohyola the accursed
Louhi grinds out provisions on the Sampo. Our children
cry for food, and their welfare is eternal!'*

". *'Well,'* Vainomoinen cried, stroking his long iron-
gray beard, *'I see but one thing to do. Louhi cheated*

*you. We will prepare an expedition of warriors and go to Pohyola and demand that she share her bounty with us!'*

" 'Louhi won't,' Ilmarinen said bitterly. *'She is a greedy hag. Her soul is black with it. Greedy for power and unending wealth.'*

" *'Then we will snatch the Star Mill away from such an abnormal creature!'* Vainomoinen cried wrathfully. *'By Hiisi, I shall take that wily witch by her long nose and—'*

" *'Calm, old friend. Let us set about our preparation for the journey. I will find Lemminkainen, the Golden Apple of Ilmatar, wherever he is wenching—and all three of us will journey to the misty island. In ships, with a thousand men!'*

"The adventures of the three heroes were strange and many but at last their seventy ships and more than three thousand warriors—for others, hearing of the great expedition and the prize, joined in—landed on the befogged coast of Pohja. Louhi, out of pride and malicious bravado, prepared a great feast for them in her black castle. While they feasted and drank the lavish spread, Ilmarinen suggested that Vainomoinen play his *kantele* and sing for them all. Vainomoinen, nothing loath, sang. But he wove his wizardry into his songs and presently Louhi and all of her household fell into a deep sleep. While they slept the three heroes pinned down their eyelids with magic needles. Then they set about finding the Star Mill where the Witch had hidden it.

"They found it in the bowels of a copper mountain, under subtle locks. It took all of Vainomoinen's wizardpower to open them and prevent the shrieking alarms with which they had been equipped. Then, carrying the Sampo to the lead ship, they embarked and Ilmarinen prayed to the winds and to Ahto, the master of all waters, to speed them on their way home.

"Storm-demons roused Louhi from her deep slumber. When she discovered that the locks had been broken and the Sampo taken, she shrieked her vengeance all the way to the Black Nebula. Her fury was terrible to behold, so that all quailed and fled, lest she take it out on those within her reach. Gathering up her best magic, she created a dreadful storm, to lash across the broad sea and strike the heroes' ships. She woke even Iku-Turso, unspeakable son of Aijo, from his mindless sleep at the bottom of the sea where he lurked in hiding from Jumala. Iku-Turso lifted his hideous head out of the water and blew his breath at the Sampo Expedition so that many of the ships floundered and sank. She caused the Mist-Maiden to weave a dense fog across the ocean so that the heroes' ship became separated from the rest.

"When the three heroes saw Iku-Turso they shivered with unspeakable dread. Even brash Lemminkainen, the golden youth, shivered and cried out for his mother, Ilmatar, Creatrix of the Universe, to save them. But Vainomoinen, of the ancient bones, knew the Word of Origin. He related to Iku-Turso, son of Aijo, of his monstrous beginnings on far forgotten stars, of his monstrous race being destroyed by Jumala, of he alone escaping to this modest uninhabited planet of molten fire. The Word of Origin did its work before Iku-Turso's hideous breath could destroy them all: he sank back to his lurk-place at the earth's center, lest Jumala find him, too.

"Louhi had meanwhile equipped a great armada of war vessels to pursue the heroes and bring back the Star Mill. The fog was so heavy that Ilmarinen's ships lost their way, drifting in aimless fashion on the black benighted seas. Louhi found them. There was a great battle.

The thousands of warriors fought. Bravely. But in the end it was magic against magic. Vainomoinen against Louhi.

"Louhi took the form of a great black eagle, swooping down to flap her great wings and cackle her fury from the ship's masthead.

"Ilmarinen sprang in front of the Sampo with his silver crossbow, Lemminkainen with his sword, while old Vainomoinen, in his curious robes, lingered at the back of it, singing the magic that would keep the witch at bay.

" 'Louhi!' Ilmarinen cried. 'I am the one who forged this Star Mill. I did not get paid for my work!'

" 'My daughter was yours for the taking!' screamed the witch. 'She still is. What more do you want?'

" 'Can we not share this wonderful thing? Surely there is enough within it for all, since it's powers of creation are endless!'

" 'Never! Never! I'll not divide the Sampo with anyone! It's mine—mine alone!' "

Kaleva paused in his story, letting his quivering hands drop to his lap. While he coughed and shuddered from his exertions and the weight of unknown years rattling those brittle bones, Ilmar stood up and paced. He stared up at the fading but still-vivid tapestry of Ilmarinen, the Wondersmith. The smith, in the tapestry, was pictured at his forge. Like Ilmar's, his short well-trimmed beard was of curling copper, his eyes space-blue but iced with wintry stars. Unlike the wizard's gorgeous trappings which Vainomoinen wore, holding his *kantele*, stroking its magical strings while he sang songs of great portent—or Lemminkainen, the handsome, beardless, golden-haired youth, shown smiling in the midst of battle—Ilmarinen was grimly intent on drawing a flaming sword out of a cauldron whose surface was a dazzling spectrum of dancing color.

Behind Ilmar, while he squinted up at what looked like himself tripled in the tapestry, Kaleva was pontificating.

"Greed is the greatest sin, because it leads to all the others. Conquest of individuals or worlds. Coveting what another has. Murder, carnage, to satisfy it. It shrivels the soul and takes away all that is honorable in a man."

Ilmar whirled, flexing his shoulders in impatience.

"What happened to the Star Mill?"

"The conflict between Vainomoinen and the Witch carried it far up in the air. It fell from Louhi's eagle-claws. It was presumed to have been broken into a million pieces and lost to the world forever."

"But it wasn't?"

"No. It was damaged, twisted into a grotesque mass of rainbow-color and alien metal—but Louhi returned after the wild storm to the spot where it vanished. She retrieved it, and by her own wicked sorcery she made it work again. But in *reversel* It can no longer absorb molecules out of space and create things from them. All it can do is destroy. Whatever comes within its domination is seized and shredded into molecular matter of a destructive nature."

Ilmar whistled.

"The Black Storm!"

"Yes. Many centuries ago Louhi set it to work out among the stars, hoping to make it the treasure-house it was before it fell. But Louhi's magic is black and evil. What came out as eternal bounty with Ilmarinen, came out in reverse, when impelled by her blasphemous sorcery. Ironically, Louhi found herself and her storm-haunted island trapped in the middle of it!"

Ilmar cracked a bony fist into his palm. "You mean that she set it into motion, only to find that it destroyed by atomic fission—and Pohyola is trapped inside because the Star Mill is still on it!"

Kaleva nodded. "Her magic is sufficient to save the witch-worldlet, but not to free herself. Yet the Storm grows and grows. If the Sampo is not destroyed—"

"It will devour the universe!" Ilmar shouted. "But if we know all this—why aren't we doing something about it? Instead of skulking down here in our educated mole-hole, why aren't we out telling the Ussi?"

Kaleva took off his blue glasses and wiped his rheumy pale eyes. "Do you think they would believe us?"

"Some of them might! We should try!"

Kaleva shivered. His bowed shoulders seemed to be holding up a terrible burden. "From time to time we have sent our spies out into the Cities, to try and find at least one Ussi we could trust. You ought to know, Ilmar, since you were one of them! All of our hopes were negative. The Ussi would not believe us, only confuse and exploit our young people. No, Ilmar, in the end we put our trust where it was always intended. In the Flame Sword that Ilmarinen created to destroy the Sampo. And—"

"And?" Ilmar demanded.

Kaleva's gentle eyes held him in a net.

"*You*, Ilmar."

## IX

ILMAR's mind was a seething maelstrom. He had made so many futile grabs at memory, battering uselessly at those locked doors so long, that when the floodgates finally were opened by this gentle dying man it was like a nova exploding inside of his skull.

The Star Mill did exist.

The Black Storm was caused by its perversion to witch's evil.

He—Ilmarinen's long-awaited time son—was destined to destroy this horror.

He found Kaleva's eyes on him, sad, thoughtful. Ilmar got up fast, impelled by the storm within him. He prowled the circumference of the round room in great strides.

"Won't the song-magic do it? Destroy the Sampo?"

"No. It has too much of the Power within it. Only another Ilmarinen, wielding another Thing of all-power, can remove what the wondersmith created."

Ilmar's hand flashed to the sword-brand on his face. "I—I tried! I already tried to get to Pohyola and destroy the Sampo!"

"It was a rash mistake, Ilmar. An overwhelming impulse must have come over you when you were out in the Cities. A chance to stowaway in a Moonship and—"

"Yes! After that into Deep. I stole a smaller ship and sent it hellbent into the heart of the Storm! I—" Ilmar snapped shut his eyes. The rag of memory was gone.

"You encountered Louhi herself?"

"I must have," Ilmar grimaced. "But I don't know what happened. If only I could remember!"

"Never mind. We must be thankful that she could not kill you, that you somehow managed to get back out to that rock where you were picked up. Ukko was with you."

Ilmar flung himself down in the ivory seat. "What about the Flame Sword? Where does that come in?"

The old man's eyes were closed. His faltering hands took hold of the long staff of rune-carved oak, his badge of leadership. His lips quivered under the swan-white beard. It was as if he prayed to the old gods for strength. For time . . .

Ilmar moved to touch his sleeve gently.

The soft eyes opened.

"That sword on your face is to tell us that our long wait is ended. It is to remind you of what Ilmarinen did, after. He was afraid, filled with remorse at what he had created. Even without knowing what Louhi had done, Ilmarinen realized what an evil Force he had unleashed; just as the Vanhat realize what their song-power is capable of in the wrong hands, Ilmarinen knew. He tried to find the Sampo. It was gone. So now Ilmarinen dedicated the rest of his life to creating a counter-force to destroy it. Hidden from the world, he sought every fragment of Otava metal which had long been used as amulets throughout the northlands. Then he secreted himself underground and went to work on the Flame Sword. And, so that this Sword could not be employed by anyone else for evil purposes, he sealed it up in such a way that only a son of his could draw it and wield it and its terrible power!"

Kaleva's fit of coughing sent him shuddering down on the couch. Ilmar sprang up to help him but the patriarch waved him away.

"Nothing can be done," he choked out. "My time is long overdue. Koulema and the black swan hold no terrors for me." His words were strangled in his own blood that spewed out of his mouth onto his white beard.

Ilmar grasped the mammoth's tusk arms of his chair in empathetic pain. He waited. Then he could not wait any longer. He must know! He must know before it was too late! Only Kaleva possessed all of the secrets!

"Where is it?" he cried. "Where is the Flame Sword?"

No answer. Kaleva lifted his skull-face and stared at Ilmar with eyes that seemed to be seeing beyond the chamber. With a convulsive motion he wrenched up on his feet. He swayed there like a wild spectre for a moment.

"Ilmar!" he rasped out, with a final futile grab at life.

"Find it—go—" His hand jerked the runic staff up and waved it. For a tick that stopped time the brandished staff seemed to point, then it dropped with a clatter.

Kaleva's funeral was a simple ritual and it was accomplished with unshed tears. All of the Vanhat, old and young, gathered on the shores of the wide Underearth lake. Old songs were chanted, and old prayers to ancient gods. Then, in grave silence, a small black barge moved out of the blue-gray mists that shrouded the far end of the lake and the unseen rock behind it. A muffled figure in gray dipped his pole into the black water to make a small sound as the barge moved out of the mist and slowly toward the waiting Vanhat.

A long box of rowanwood, on which was draped the Vanhat flag—space-blue with a dipper of silver stars—was placed on the brief dock. The ferryman in the gray shroud brought the barge to the wooden pier and moored it. Ilmar's skin crawled when the tall cowled figure turned momentarily for a look that included all in the watching ring of faces. The face within the gray cowl was veiled heavily, so that no expression could be detected, yet the slow look seemed to express friendly foreboding. The ferryman moved then. He lifted the coffin easily to his shoulder and lowered it onto his barge.

Silence. Deep silence. Then, again, the gentle thrusting sound of his pole into the black water. As the barge moved across the somber lake and into the mist, faintly, so very faintly that it might have come from a far-off star, Ilmar heard the black swan singing. Its farewell floated sweetly across the dark water, then dwindled gently away to tug one along with it, while the blue-gray mists took Kaleva and the barge and the strange ferryman into their keeping.

The loss was sharp for them all. After nearly two hundred years, Kaleva seemed incapable of ever leaving them. Yet, the reaction to the loss of their leader expressed itself oddly: instead of numb panic, each of the Vanhat felt it his unspoken duty to work harder, to be kinder, to make up to each one of the others for his great loss. As otherwhere, when disaster strikes, individual problems were thrust out of sight.

Ilmar could not do this.

Not quite.

His problem was too all-consuming. Too vital.

The gentle bondage which the Vanhat lived under, here in Underearth, was something he could not quite take. Kaleva, out of gentle understanding, his simple magnificence, his empathy for all men, had imprinted their minds with their silken bondage. Obscure to most, their duty was to have angelic patience until the time must come when they might move out into the sun and join the rest of the human race.

Kaleva's philosophies were evident everywhere; his ideas were like crystal-clear mountain streams that flow out of the eternal snows into the muddy rivers inhabited by predatory fish, big ones devouring little.

Kaleva's revelations had relieved his need to know, yes, but they had also inspired bigger questions—and the fierce need for action. They had waited for him to be born so that he might destroy the potential destroyer of *everything*. They looked to him, with their side-glances and silences, when he tried to be casually friendly or to ask what any of them knew about the Flame Sword. They knew nothing, but their attitude was one of confident respect. Ilmar would find a way. Kaleva had said it.

What a legacy! What a thing to dump in his lap!

At night, when he finally managed to find sleep, he

began to have dreams. Dreams of his childhood. Of Nyyrikki . . .

Ilmar was ten, Nyyrikki eleven. They had sneaked up to the entrance of the Rare Earth mines—the ancient mine-mouth which led to Lake Imari and the village. Other times they had only peeked out between the rotting boards, made purposely uninteresting and unimportant, for the rare cases when the Illusion machine that was taped with old songs and created the barrier between their valley and the Ussi, might fail temporarily. It had happened. The villagers took care of it in a naïve bumbling way. The Ussi aircraft (it was invariably by air that the valley was spotted) would land because of some error or mechanical failure and the villagers would just "happen" to have parts of wrecked aircraft that would put them on their way.

This time Nyyrikki had brought a gun, a rifle taken from the Museum. He'd cleaned and loaded it. Although there was no need for fresh meat, since the Vanhat grew most of their food in hydroponic tanks, Nyyrikki craved it and was bound to enjoy the thrill of stalking and killing. His description of how they would skin their prize and cook it over an open fire was irresistible. Ilmar had adventure in his bones, too.

"But when Kaleva finds out!"

"So what? Aino will lie for us." Nyyrikki guffawed. "For you she would do anything."

"Kaleva always finds out," Ilmar said. "We will be punished."

"Extra work?" Nyyrikki hooted. "Forbid us the night-sings for a week? This is worth it, Fire-Face!"

From the mine-mouth Ilmar stared out widely at the open sky. It was so huge—so real. It made him dizzy to look up into it, as if he might fall upwards into all that nothing. He stared at the sun in frozen rapture until it burned dazzles on his brain.

Nyyrikki's hand shook him from this ecstasy.

"Hurry up, stupid! Some old biddy from the village will spot us in these clothes!"

With a gulp, Ilmar tumbled after him into the woods. The sunspots still burned his eyes, but the pain itself was a joy. To see the sky and the pale winking stars of summer half-night. Ilmar's yearning outstripped Nyyrikki's. It sprang from his soul, not his belly.

Their boys' game of being ancient hunters like in the old songs carried them through the fragrant pines and pungent cedars, across the rusted forest floor, at a gallop. The rich scents of humus and needles made Ilmar want to shout in delirious happiness. He touched the rough barks and chewed on needles. He was of it all, of the southwind soughing above them, of the swallows chattering in the lacy emerald glades. This was Tapiola. Magic Tapiola.

A fat rodent nosed out of his hole. It waddled up on a rotted log for an unabashed look. Nyyrikki lifted the rifle to his shoulder. Ilmar yelled and bumped against his arm. The rifle cracked, shivering the trees around them.

"They'll hear the shot, Nyy! These old guns made a heck of a noise!"

Nyyrikki whirled savagely. "You made me miss, damn you! Now he's gone!"

"Woodchucks are no good to eat."

"How do you know?"

"If you read your lessons once in a while—"

"Shut up, Sword-Face!"

They moved on in silence. Ilmar was so captivated by the sights and small sounds and the smells that he hardly noticed that Nyyrikki, stalking ahead, stopped short with a gasp for quiet. Ilmar blinked. In a pool of golden sunlight where motes danced, stood a deer. A magnificent buck with ten-point antlers. A forest god! Tapio himself!

Nyyrikki drew a careful bead, but the animal stood there, head raised, proud, fearless. While Nyyrikki's aim wavered the stag dropped pose. Then he went back to the business of scraping winter shag from his antlers on a lightning-felled pine.

The inviolable rule among the Vanhat was: Never kill for sport, only for food. To kill such a magnificent beast as this caught Ilmar's breath up. They couldn't eat it. They couldn't give it to the Day's villagers. . . .

Ilmar was back too far to do anything but shout "No!" but some extra-sensory warning clove his tongue to the roof of his mouth. By what he had done and was doing, Nyyrikki was trying to prove something. His worth to the Vanhat? His bravery?

Behind them a small other sound snapped the hush.

The stag faltered wonderingly. Then fell with a great crash.

Nyyrikki whirled. "Ilmar! I didn't! I didn't do it!"

"That's right, boy. I did."

The voice behind them wore a chuckle of self-gratification. They turned in sudden panic. The words were Ussi! And as the man in hunter's clothes swaggered up, his fleshy face revealed a craving and delight in killing; it was there in his pinched pale eyes, in the curve of his flabby lips.

They could only stare in wonder. They had never seen an Ussi.

"Your gun makes hardly any sound," Nyyrikki blurted.

"Sure drops them though, eh?" The hunter grinned. "Finds the target every time."

"Then why—" Ilmar stopped short, biting his lip.

Nyyrikki caught his glance. Where was the sport of it if the bullet never missed? But the hunter wasn't paying attention to them now. He was examining his kill, smiling. The stag's eyes were glazing over, dull and unseeing as his blood warmed the new shoots of green, the crocuses.

The stranger put a proprietary foot on his prize and started bragging about his other kills, not only on Mars and Venus, but in Deep. "The man-like primitives are best. They give you a real fight."

"How did you get here into our valley?" Ilmar asked.

"Damn little hunting here on Terra, but I was told that bear and deer had been sighted up here in the Lake Imari district. I was warned about the storms, but hell. And just where did you come from? I didn't see you down in the village. What's those clothes you're wearing?"

Kaleva's law was: *Ussi must never know.*

"We are from the village," Ilmar said.

"Hell! In these synthetics? The villagers fixing my plane talk like inbred morons. Haven't got the brains to go south into the Cities." He lifted his strange rifle-size weapon. "I've heard some funny stuff about this lake region. Another man whose plane crashed up here in a storm like I did—he said some wild things. Sent a patrol up here to investigate, but they couldn't locate the valley."

Ilmar's mind raced. What to do? They weren't supposed to be up on the surface at all. Now this Ussi, this rich hunter. But Nyyrikki moved first.

He fell on his knees, groveling. "Don't kill us! We'll tell you who we are. We'll take you to our underground city!"

The hunter's eyes went wide and the gun sagged.

"Nyyrikki!" Ilmar yelled. "What are you do—"

Nyyrikki whirled on him. "Shut! Can't you see the

great hunter has us where he wants us? His gun can't
miss, stupid!"

But when the strange weapon the hunter's pudgy
hands gripped dropped to his side, Nyyrikki moved like
summer lightning. His rifle swung up and crackled fire.
The Ussi hunter wore a hole in his forehead that didn't
belong, and a surprised look, as he toppled across the
dead stag.

Ilmar bolted up from his childhood dream. This was
memory flooding back, sharp, cogent, important. His
first brush with an Ussi and, unhappily, a poor specimen.
His poignant memory of friendship with Nyyrikki. This
one episode was branded more deeply on his mind than
all of the others.

He smiled grimly, remembering the follow-up.

Kaleva was glacial; sterner than at any other time
Ilmar had seen him. Nyyrikki had created a crisis which
had forced him to transgress a vital Vanhat law. He
had killed. And Ilmar was party to the crime. Kaleva's
blue eyes burned into Ilmar's brain.

"You are more to blame than Nyyrikki!"

"Me!"

"Yes. You know what is right. While Nyyrikki . . ."
The ancient sighed deep. "You are old enough to know
his secret."

"Secret!"

"Remember the old songs of Kullervo?"

"He was forced to wander the cold wastes forever, because of a terrible sin he committed. There was an evil
seed in his blood. He—" Ilmar stopped with a breath-
held gulp.

Kaleva nodded somberly. "Yes, Ilmar. Kullervo's fate
was bitter. And Nyyrikki bears the taint. This is the
thing he must battle for the whole of his rash life; this

is the thing which inspires his wildness. When you two
go out into the Ussi world in secret, it must be *you* who
leads; you, Ilmar. You must keep faith when Nyyrikki's
evil seed becomes too strong for him."

The lesson was clean-cut. Ilmar must help Nyyrikki,
bend him to wiser paths when the wildness took hold of
him. Ilmar should be wary when Nyyrikki went too far.
Ilmar must teach Nyyrikki, guide him.

Yet, in the end, it was Nyyrikki who taught Ilmar.

Taught him how a man dies.

## X

EACH DAY that passed was a frustration. Lost time. Self
torment. Kaleva had put a burden on Ilmar, or rather
reinforced the burden Ilmar saw written on his face
every time he trimmed his colorful beard. Even to glance
into a mirror or to pass by a curve of polished steel was
agony.

He prowled the deepest caves like an animal. He must
find the Flame Sword. And the Gate. But—where?
Where?

He couldn't eat or sleep. He gave up trimming his
beard and shunned reflecting metals like a vampire.
When sleep did come to him it brought dreams of the
Witch on the high crag, cackling and mocking him, dar-
ing him to try again.

*"Ilmarinen couldn't defeat me, so how can his spawn?
But come to Pohyola! Try! My demon dogs are hungry!"*

Lokka found him haggardly wandering the halls, mumbling to himself. She led him to her rooms, where she
forced him to eat.

"I can't, Mother!"

"Drink, then. It will give you strength. You must put

meat back on those bones if you are to replace Kaleva and be our new leader."

"Leader!" Ilmar jammed his finger at the fire-mark on his cheek. "With *this!* You know I can't rest until this brand is gone. And you know what will make it be gone!"

"Listen, Ilmar. I have prepared a cosmetic paste. I learned it from reading Ussi books. It's really wonderful. It will cover anything and practically becomes a part of your skin. Here! Look! Let me put just a little on—"

Ilmar glowered down at the jar. His impulse to send it skittering across the chamber dwindled at the beseeching look in her eyes.

"I know what you're trying to do, Mother. But it's no use." His head fell to his arms, on the table. He shuddered from exhaustion.

He felt Lokka's work-worn hands tremble across his coppery head. "Ilmar, we must have a Leader. You are the one. If you should leave and never come back—what shall we do?"

Ilmar sighed, pulling himself up. "I want to, Mother—but how can I? If I neglected my task I would not be worthy to lead the Vanhat. How can you ask?"

"I can," Lokka said. "I can ask it. So can Aino."

Something in her voice stiffened his muscles; he whirled sharply. "You're not holding something back from me, Mother. Something I should know?"

She shook her head, avoided his look.

"You're sure Kaleva didn't tell you something, in case he died very suddenly—"

"No. He told me nothing."

Ilmar stood up quickly. He moved and took hold of Lokka's bony shoulders, firmly, gently. He looked deep in her eyes. "It's Aino, isn't it."

"I don't know, my son. But I—I believe that Kaleva

would not want a mother to be the one who sent her own son to die."

Aino was spy-trained. She had learned the art of wide-eyed duplicity, a rare thing among the Vanhat. She used it now. When Ilmar shook her by the shoulders and demanded what she knew, her innocence was worthy of Pohyola's daughter herself.

"I don't know a thing, *rakas*. Not a thing. How should Kaleva tell me? He knows that I love you more than my life."

Ilmar swore through tight lips. "I am not at all convinced. You're the logical one for him to tell." He kissed her savagely, then pushed her back. "One more time, Aino. If you lie to me now, you know that I can never respect you again." He waited, while Aino crushed herself against him, sobbing.

"I—don't—know—anything."

Ilmar brushed away from her. "Don't you care about all the people who have been killed? The billions who will be? Nyyrikki . . ."

Aino's eyes flashed. "I only care about us, Ilmar. You tried once. Whatever happens—it's a slow thing. The Storm feeds slowly. It's so far away. In our lifetime—"

Ilmar tossed her a grim look and started out of her room.

"Wait!" she sobbed, harshly.

He froze, turned.

"Kaleva didn't tell me anything, not really. But once, when he heard that you were to be killed by the Ussi and his heart collapsed, he said one thing to me. It doesn't mean much."

"What did he say?" Ilmar demanded.

"He said: *If I die and if Jumala spares Ilmar, tell him that the Sword is where it is and the Gate is behind it.*"

Ilmar took Aino in his arms and kissed her. But it was

not until his steps led him without conscious direction toward Kaleva's round sanctum and his fingers closed around the handle to open the door that he *knew*. The tapestried chamber had been left closed, like a shrine, in the weeks since Kaleva had died. It was for the new Leader of the Vanhat to reopen it. Ilmar had turned his back on leadership, out of guiltful need for action. His task came first. The stigmata on his face must be erased.

He moved purposefully across the thin patina of dust, past the couch with Kaleva's runic staff on it. Now he knew. He knew exactly what Kaleva had tried to do, with his last remaining shred of life. He had flailed out his staff, kinetically the staff itself had whipped up in his feeble grasp—and pointed.

At the tapestry of Ilmarinen, the Wondersmith.

Ilmarinen drawing out the Flame Sword.

*The Sword is where the Sword is.*

When he reached the silk-and-gold cloth, the enormous Ilmarinen of the copper beard and determined eyes, Ilmar stopped. He looked up at his ancestor, his father by some curious Time-fold. In the uncertain light the giant figure seemed on the very point of moving. Of actually drawing the Sword out of the cauldron the rest of the way.

In the breathless silence, the Wondersmith seemed on the hairpoint of speech.

"*Take the Sword,*" the looming giant told him. "*It fits your hand. No one else's. Your blood is in it.*"

Ilmar moved a step closer. Another. Now the warp and woof of the skillfully loomed cloth was close enough for him to reach out and touch. The tapestry texture felt coarse to his roving fingers, from the copper and brass and gold threads that had been woven into it; from the reeds and grasses; from the strange red and blue dyes, like blood, like mineral clay.

"I can't reach it." Ilmar grinned up at the woven giant.

*"Try. Try with all of your mind."*

Ilmar shrugged. He crabbed his fingers up the rough fabric. Up. Up. He strained his hand toward the Sword's hilt. When the uselessness of attempting to reach a ten-foot sword down from ten yards over his head struck him, the Sword seemed to retreat. When he gritted his teeth, closed his eyes, saw it dwindle and move downward in his mind—it did.

"Ouch!"

The flame scorched his hand before his fist gripped the hilt Ilmarinen handed him. Touching the blue-fire sapphire set in the hilt sent a thrill of new blood spinning through him, through every capillary, every minor nerve. It was like touching Ilmarinen's soul.

*"Put it in your belt,"* the Wondersmith's voice whispered out of Time.

"I have no sheath."

*"Try. Perkele, boy! It took me ten years of my last heart's blood to fashion it! Take it!"*

Ilmar curved his fingers around the hilt. It was like grasping Ilmarinen's own steel-tough hand. He lowered the Flame Sword to his wide belt doubtfully. But the Sword knew it belonged there. It whipped around him three times, like a thing alive, concealing itself in his thick leather belt. By turns it was short, then long. When it found its home the tip of it dug through Ilmar's forest-green tunic and found his spine. It pinpricked in his flesh and remained there.

Ilmar winced, but wonder was uppermost. He looked up at Ilmarinen. The Wondersmith seemed to smile now.

"The Gate?" Ilmar asked.

*"Behind this rag, of course!"* A freezing wind out of space itself billowed the tapestry. *"Ukko! Do I have to tell you everything?"*

## PART THREE

## THE STAR MILL

"Ukko, thou of gods the highest,
Give me here a Sword of Fire,
By a sheath of fire protected,
That I may resist misfortune,
And I may avoid destruction,
Overcome the powers of evil . . ."

KALEVALA: *Runo X*

## XI

WHAT THE GATE was on the other side was blurred by
eternal mystery, but on this side the gate was made out
of wood and it sagged rather badly. The high pickets had
been painted blue but most of the color was gone now
so that mostly weathered gray wood showed on the log
posts, the gate itself, and the length of the long sloped
fence on both sides of it.

Ilmar replaced the oval of heavy wire carefully on the
pickets after creaking it shut behind him. He stared
back where he had come from, but it wasn't as it had
been. Now it was deep green forest. He turned.

Across a wide meadow a cock crowed.

Ilmar shaded his eyes along the down-sweep of har-
vested rye stubble to the red barns and stables of the
farmyard; he pushed his wondering look further, where,
within the rear courtyard the land rose again, leading
across hand-pump and kitchens to the dark castle itself.
He gaped, listening to the sounds of the farm's awaken-
ing; the soft hungry lowing of bullocks, the bleat of
newly weaned lambs, the squealing grunt of hogs as
the slop-mash sloshed into their troughs. Predawn on a
castle farm.

Ilmar's eyes carried him up into the foggy sky, while
the leap of wonder at all of this strangely prosaic magic
flung itself through his lanky frame. Overhead a hawk
moved in lopsided circles against the gray-black smear;
he, too, was searching out his breakfast in the wide
meadow's bowl.

Stared out, Ilmar sat himself down on a big boulder
to try and assimilate all about him, to place himself into
it, to orient himself. The boulder was smooth on top. A

thousand times Louhi's farm slaves had stolen a moment of rest on it, snatching a breather from humdrum drudgery. Beyond the picket fence, where he *ought* to have come from, was a charred spot, remnant of a thousand nightly fire-sings. Barren places in the sward and gathered rocks and bits of log from the forest encircled the dead fire. The forest back of the fire-sing-place lifted shaggy and dense with pine and fir and spruce. Still further, where the forest lifted onto high ground, a rocky cliff reared up into the mists.

Ilmar drank in the autumn tang, the waking hunger of the farm, the hawk's piercing invocation, the witch castle looming under alien suns; he was dizzy and unsure of himself. It would have been well to have brought some kind of weapon of Ussi manufacture. Yet, would such a weapon work against star-demons?

He blinked up at the tower. There was a small slash of window where the dark mist began to thicken into the consistency and color of diseased liver. Straining his eyes, he thought he detected a flicker of movement. A corbie or crow, perhaps?

Until this morning his only concern had been to get here with the Flame Sword. But now that he was here on Louhi's peripatetic worldlet, what next? Sorcery and cunning were the Witch's watchwords. Louhi's evil nature was so strong that it soaked up all of the other evil in the universe like a sponge, and had done so for thousands of years. Her pacts with alien creatures who were inimical to man had given her immense power.

Ilmar had no such powers and even Ukko shunned this plague spot in the galaxy. True, he had Ilmarinen's Sword—but that had been designed for one purpose only. To destroy the Sampo. There was nothing to prevent Louhi from destroying him before he could reach it, or even locate it. She would naturally have hidden the Star Mill in some secret spot, well protected by daemonaic device.

What to do?

A sigh and a wild roving glance gave him a shred of an idea. The Gate! On this side it was a typical farm gate designed to keep farm animals in and forest beasts out. So. Ilmar must assume a role. He would be an early hunter returned empty-handed; somehow he would conceal himself among Louhi's army of slaves. The Gate had been contrived to this end!

*"Paiva."*

The civil greeting came from behind a hummock across the narrow barnyard path. Ilmar turned with a start. His eyes went wide to see a bush of green-brown hair moving above the barley stalks. Then a pair of enormous round eyes like animate emeralds.

*"Paiva,* elf," Ilmar returned.

There was a high titter, and the barley stalks whisked aside. Ilmar found himself staring at an oversize alien head, round, greenish in color, smallmouthed, but with a pair of large fluted ears that oscillated and swiveled in bewildering fashion. It appeared that the small alien's globular head appendages were in constant undulating movement, more so when he was excited, and that functionally and organically they were far more than just ears.

"I'm not an elf, cousin!"

Ilmar grinned. The creature could not have measured more than two foot six, from the tips of his upturned brown leather sandals with the bells on the toes, to that verdant plethora of grasshopper-spit hair. In fact, there was something of a grasshopper about the folded manner in which his spindly arms and legs were attached to his pear-shaped torso. He wore a bright yellow suit of silk, with a wide scalloped collar around his stick of a neck, and there were bells dangling from the points of his collar and his elbows as well.

"For that matter," Ilmar said good-naturedly, "I'm not your cousin, elf!"

The gooseberry eyes protruded in surprise.

"You've got to be!"

"Be what?" Ilmar forced himself not to laugh. The little alien's forehead was suddenly rutted by a ludicrous, painful frown. There was something ingenuously appealing about him; Ilmar warmed to him as to one of Tapio's small furry creatures out of the wood.

"Karina's cousin, Toivo from over the mountain, of course!"

"Must I?"

"Who else *could* you be?" The little one waved his arms in desperation, setting the bells to jingling.

Ilmar shrugged and stood up. "Well, if I must, I must. By the way, who are you?"

A pleased titter, then the alien held his breath before he said, "*Kokokokokokokokokokokoko.*"

Ilmar smiled and nodded. "*Niin.* I understand. You are called that because you are the one who 'gathers up all the firewood and stacks it in a pile by the fire.' "

The ears flapped wildly. "The Mistress named me so because one of my duties is to tend her fireplace up in the Tower. I do lots of other things for her, too. I run and fetch things. I bring the sweet cakes every morn—"

"Never mind the rundown. I'll just call you Koko. Okay?"

Koko hopped back and forth in great glee. From the get-up, Ilmar decided that the Mistress of Pohyola kept the little alien around her mainly as her court jester.

"Let's go find Karina, Cousin Toivo. She will give us a caraway cake and a pitcher of fresh milk." His seven-fingered hand crept confidently into Ilmar's and tugged him down the cowpath.

"Why do you keep calling me 'Cousin Toivo'?"

"Because you *are*. But if you don't want the Mistress to know you've come back, I won't tell."

"Thank you, Koko." As they moved toward the barns and the circular rear courtyard of the Castle, Ilmar said lightly, "Then you know where I came from?"

"Sure, Cousin Toivo. Everybody in the Castle knows *that*. You were hiding in the caves behind Turtle Mountain, with all the other slaves who ran off eight years ago. The Mistress posted her best archers at the top of the mountain, to pick off the rebels whenever any of them poked his nose out to find food. You were just a boy when you joined the slave-rebels, so my Mistress said not to kill you. That's what she told Karina. She said it was all right for you to come back. And here you are!"

"Here I am," Ilmar echoed.

They moved around the barns and across the flagged court to the bake-house, next to the kitchen. A girl wearing a dark blue skirt and white apron, with a white kerchief framing her flour-daubed face, was in the act of pulling great round rye breads out of the great stone-and-clay bake oven with a long wooden spatula and adding them to the neat rows on a nearby table. Ilmar sniffed hungrily at the savory odor of the fresh loaves.

Koko hopped in, babbling excitedly. The girl gave him a swift side-glance while she kept at her task. In the doorway, Ilmar saw that Karina was pretty but not artfully pretty. She was healthy-pretty, with her womanly breasts heaving a little beneath the drawstring blouse that lopped down over one sturdy shoulder. Dark hair clung to her beaded forehead, strayed from under the kerchief; her round cheeks were rosy under the flour-smears, from her bristling activity.

"Tell our Mistress she will have to wait for her special milk-cakes," she snapped. "You're early, and besides—"

"Karina!" Koko shrilled, plucking her skirt. "Look who's with me! I found him sitting on a rock near the forest!"

"I haven't time for nonsense, Koko. Can't you see that I—"

When her hazel eyes swept over Koko's pointed head, she saw Ilmar. Her scowl vanished. She stared, wide-eyed.

"Who—who are you?"

Koko danced up and down, tittering, bells tinkling. "Don't you know your own Cousin?"

The girl's red lips tightened; her green-brown eyes flicked over Ilmar's green synthetics tunic to his copper-red beard and froze on his deep blue eyes.

"You are not Toivo!" she blurted.

Ilmar went over to her and kissed her cheek. "That's no wonder, Karina. Toivo was only a boy eight years ago. Living on mushrooms and roots—" His fingers squeezed her hand while he went on improvising, cutting off further protest.

Karina gasped, blinking away tears. There was something rare and strange in the redbeard's eyes; she must not say the wrong thing. She grabbed up a wooden bucket and handed it to Koko.

"Be a good boy and fetch some water from the well. Pump it fresh."

"But the trough in the corner is full!" he grumbled.

"Fresh water. For our *virras*."

"He's no *virras*. He's Cousin Toivo from—"

"Scoot! And on the way back stop at the kitchen for

a pitcher of warm milk. But not a word about Toivo, understand?"

Koko accepted the chore with a grimace. Ilmar watched him hop-skip down the stone flagging in the direction of the central well; other servants in drab homespun of primitive cut were yawning about their morning tasks. Karina closed the door briskly, pointing Ilmar to seat himself at the uncluttered end of the long worktable. While she talked she finished unloading the great stone and mud-brick ovens.

"He won't be able to keep his mouth shut for long, I'm afraid." She faced him wistfully. "Cousin Toivo, I just can't believe you're here. The Mistress promised to spare you, but I still can't believe . . ."

"Listen, Karina—believe. Believe that I am Cousin Toivo, at least for now. But don't think about it too hard. Tell me things I must know."

When she handed him a loaf and a kitchen *pukko* to cut it with, along with a wedge of yellow cheese, her hand trembled.

"Eat, Toivo. You look starved." Back at her morning chore, she added, with a rush, "The Mistress' powers are dim this early. Her body is sluggish until she re-fortifies her magic. It will be expected that I should hide my cousin from her as long as possible."

"Koko?"

"He will not betray you, but he loves to talk. His race is kind but simple. They have a great need to be loved and admired. He will not be able to restrain himself from babbling about you when he brings Louhi her morning cakes."

Ilmar frowned.

"There is a way to stop him from babbling."

Karina turned, fearful. "You wouldn't kill Koko!"

"No. Simply hypnotism. I will remove all knowledge about me from his mind."

The girl wagged her head and clucked her tongue. "Well, you must do what you must. To have come to this terrible place without being made captive is a hero's act. Something tells me you want to help and if I can do anything that—"

Koko burst in, slopping water on the stone floor, giggling pleasure at having done a good thing. While Koko devoured his milk and cakes, Ilmar put him under simple hypnosis and removed the whole sequence of their meeting in the meadow and the rest of it from his low-caliber mind. He had met nobody on his morning ramble. Cousin Toivo hadn't come back. There would be nothing beyond everyday memories to tempt his magpie's tongue when he hopped back to the Castle with the Witch's breakfast cakes.

Karina found him a loose woolen slave's garment to wear over his Vanhat tunic; she also found him a nest in the barn loft, where he could sleep in safety among the hay sheaves. He dare not be seen by the housekeeper, a raw-boned hellion, or by any of Louhi's shrunken army of castle warriors. While Louhi's olden magic, a perversion of the Vanhat all-power, kept Pohyola on the move in the direction of Terra, she must depend for menials and defensive warriors on the progeny of those who were entrapped with her when the Black Storm first began to pour out its venom. Despair and bad treatment had reduced her armies of servitors. The lush days of the Sampo in full flower were ancient history now. *Eil* These were bad days for the Mistress of All Evil!

Ilmar lay back on his clasped hands, wishing that Karina's multiplicity of duties had permitted him time for more questions. But any divergence of routine would only tempt trouble. She would come back after the long day's work was finished and they could talk more, and plan. Karina would be his hands and his eyes until the time for action came. True, Louhi could not remove herself from the black web she had created; yet, within the confines of Pohyola itself her magic was as strong as ever.

The high loft was accessible only by ladder; everywhere, besides the small square trapdoor in the center, the loft was stacked rafter-high with sheaves of hay for the long winter snows. Louhi had created her perambulating hell's island out of terran earth and creatured it with terran creatures; it must follow that terran ways must obtain, since even the blood in the Witch's deathless body was terran in origin. Like many older Vanhat, Louhi despised Ussi technology and would have none of it. Simple cosmic evil was good enough for her.

Busy with such ponderings, Ilmar found Utamo reluctant to give him sleep; so he burrowed his way between the drying sheaves to a knothole in the ancient pine wall. Through this knothole he obtained a reasonably inclusive view of the kitchen courtyard, the stone-rimmed well with its cross-legged animal troughs, the slaves' quarters, and Karina's bake-house. He watched the slaves move dispiritedly about their tasks. Once in a while a brute-faced warrior would swagger across the packed earth court, slapping his brief leather-fringed skirt with a well-used whip. These were unsavory remnants of Louhi's plundering armies and defenders of the Castle; lack of professional exercise had reduced them to sadistic lackwits who found some outlet for their fight-trained muscles in baiting the Castle's servants.

One of these types, bigger and uglier than the rest and sporting a longer, stouter whip, made his appearance. Ilmar found himself wondering why this warrior's stocky legs were encased in thick leather boots, hip-high, and why he wore shoulder-length leather gloves. He wondered, too, why the slaves fled in all directions. Even the spindly slinker at his heels, who toted a large basket on his toil-crooked back, dropped the basket hastily when the leather-clad figure stopped, and loped like a coyote for some hole to crawl into.

The giant in leather unhatched the lock on a sheet-iron length of fence with a heavily wired top. Ilmar couldn't see what was caged behind that sheet-iron fence, but at the giant's shrill whistle and the seeming of routine daily procedure, he heard. And what he heard turned his blood to ice.

Yelping in a quasi-intelligent fashion, the demon hounds leaped out of their iron kennels. Their deep-throated screams were ululations of pure unadulterated hate; Louhi had traded these fanged horrors from their own relatives—star-demons out of the Black Nebula—removed certain of their powers to chain them to her and triple their blood-lust. They were black, Louhi's demon dogs. Black and gigantic, with muscles that quivered for the kill; with eyes like crimson swords, and fangs that could tear the heart out of a man in one great bite, after those yellow-black talons had stripped away his muscles.

They hated everything they saw. Everything represented captivity away from a planet where such monsters were routine, and had to be to survive others as bad or worse. Everything feared them. Every mouse, every wood animal burrowing into the farmyard hopeful of foodscraps, every human. When their leaps for the warrior's throat failed they loped the circumference of the courtyard in search of live kill. Finding none, they settled down with the basketful of dripping flesh-and-bones and the giant's curses for sauce.

Ilmar shivered. He knew the demon hounds; for it was they, on their night-prowls, who had thwarted his first rash attempt to find the perverted Star Mill.

## XII

FURTIVE taps on the loft's trapdoor tore apart the umbilicus between Ilmar and sleep. It was pitch-dark. Not a hint of light spun through his peephole. Pohyola's ever-fog and the Black Storm above it held back starshine and, had it not been for Louhi's witchery, would have held back the light of the alien sun as well.

Stifling a sneeze from the hay dust, Ilmar crawled through the tunnels he had fashioned to the trap. Again the knock; Karina's prearranged signal.

He lifted the trap and helped the breathless girl up. She melted against him for a long moment after he had replaced the square on the ladder-hole. Ilmar felt the wild beating of her heart under her full round breasts, with a rush of virile passion. He eased her away gently, understanding. Karina, like little Koko, suffered from an excess of love and passion and she had no peg on which to hang it. Even Toivo was gone and, Ilmar secretly thought, for good. Witch Louhi had never been one to keep her promises, nor did her vindictive spirit ever forgive. No, like the other last-ditch rebels, Toivo was long since wolf meat on the far side of Turtle Mountain. As for Karina's fellow-slaves, generations of servitude had turned them into vegetables. That last thrust for freedom had been the ultimate spark of manhood. They would never escape; even the Witch had not yet found a way to.

Yet, while despair bred stagnation, Karina was an atavist. Some fierce genetic urge within her strong well-curved body demanded resistance. She resisted the only way she could, by hard work and by making her talents indispensable to the greedy hag. To Karina, Ilmar was her Toivo still, but he must not take advantage. There was Aino to think of, and his prodigious task.

"Shall I try a light?" he asked, while they crouched among the prickling sheaves, Karina still clinging to his arm.

"Better not. All this hay."

"Where are the others?"

"At the night-sing. They're allowed one hour, so we don't have much time. Then the dogs are set free to guard the Castle." He felt her whole body shiver.

"Were you able to find out anything?"

"Nobody among the slaves has ever heard of the Sampo."

Ilmar scowled. "I'm not surprised. Where does Louhi spend most of her time these days?"

"In the Tower. She is working on a way to free herself from the island, Koko told me. He even got me up there once, so that I could plead for Toivo's life. First she only gave me that fiend's cackle, then she said that her archers would spare him, if the animals didn't get him, but he would have to make it back on his own." Her grip tightened. "Ilmar—do you think—"

He held her closer, in the curve of his arm. "Don't hope too much, Karina. It's been eight years and Louhi gloats on tortures of all kinds."

She sobbed against him for a long moment. "What—what can I do? She wants to breed me with one of her warriors, as she breeds her livestock. So far I've managed to lie about my age and keep her happy with the goodies I cook—"

Ilmar kissed her cheek. "Around the sing-fires they tell of a beautiful land of blue lakes and forests, of happy things, of heroes—of free choice!"

"These things are only dreams."

"No, Karina. They're real and I promise you one thing. If I find and destroy the Sampo I will take you back with me to taste freedom and to marry whomever you want to."

"How can you, Ilmar? How can you outwit *her?*"

"I've got to. Listen! You said the hag spends all her time in the Tower. She wouldn't keep the Star Mill far from her. It must be up there somewhere. I've got to get up there!"

"How can you, Ilmar!" she wailed. "It's guarded by a hundred warriors who will use any excuse to kill one of us. And in only a few minutes—the dogs!"

When she gasped back her fear for him, Ilmar heard an eager eldritch baying from the darkness below. Like the warriors, the demon hounds would find Ilmar a tasty tidbit. His long fingers tightened over Karina's hand.

"We must find another way up to the hag's Tower!"

"I—I have heard there is one. I'll try to find out from the slaves who do the cleaning. Then—"

"I'll meet you at the bake-house, just before dawn. When the Witch's powers are at their lowest ebb and the dogs have been returned to their kennels."

The trapdoor slid back into place behind the girl; Ilmar eased himself back for a night of fitful dozing and the dark wait. He thought about the other slaves, listening to their shuffling movements from out of the meadow and their hour's release from bondage in the old heroic songs, back to their long bunkhouses before the dogs were unleashed.

He thought about Kaleva and Nyyrikki, of Lokka—

and of Aino. Waiting. Begging Ukko and the star-powers for the boon of Ilmar back with them, alive. He thought about Captain Grant, about Joe and Brooks, and the untold thousands of starmen who had been trapped by the perverted Star Mill.

His harassed thoughts were whipped away by the alien screams of the demon dogs. Worry for Karina nagged him. Demand for action washed across his nerves, his muscles, compelling him. What time was it? He dared not sleep. Farms like Louhi's came to life when it was still half-night. He moved. He descended into the pungent barn odors and the chopping sounds of animal hooves. Vague light sifted across the hay-strewn planks, from under the double doors. He moved swiftly toward it, and cracked one side open. The alien moon was a blurred cat's eye.

He took a fast look across the wide circular yard, from the iron kennels to the stone wall, to the smoke-house and Karina's bake-house next to a double row of cordwood. Across the yard, further left, were the long shale-roofed sleep quarters.

Yes, there were plenty of black pools for the fiend-dogs to lurk in wait. But there was no sound at all. . . .

He had one weapon, a razor-sharp *pukko*—the triangular-blade knife all Finns once wore for hunting, fishing, eating. Such was his hurry that he had neglected to bring along a grip-gun; anyway, guns were useless against Louhi.

Vanhat spies were trained for animal cunning and the tracking instincts of his ancestors were retaught from deep in his genes. He moved. From shadow to shadow, with a noiseless breath-stop in between moves. Barn to shed, shed to well-trough. Here he crouched, sucking in gulps of thin night air. The woodpile was next. He would wait at the womens' quarters' door for Karina.

A low snuffling growl iced his nerves. Then he saw the two giant hounds, loping along the well-stacked pine wood, one nuzzling the other's flank. Right where he was headed!

He pulled in a silent preparatory breath.

They stopped. He saw four baleful eyes turn his way. It was as if they heard him. Or scented him, although there was no telltale wind. Not a breath. Not a scratch from a night-scavenging rodent. Those eight hounds discouraged every living thing from revealing its existence while they prowled. Ilmar saw the huge slavering jaws bare long fangs, eyes blazing at him like red hellflames.

He must have made a sound for sure, now.

Because now, with low clucking growls they leaped toward him like two black demons.

Ilmar's *pukko* struck the first one's heart in one lightning downstroke. Overconfident, it ran right into his knife. Its fangs raked his arm before it reared up, yelping surprised agony and wrath, then collapsed in a scramble of flailing legs.

Its bitch companion, out of some animal deference, had held back. Now her anger, seeing her night's partner writhing in his own hot blood, knew no bounds. She was on Ilmar with raping claws and snarling fanged mouth. He tried to leap behind the trough. He didn't quite make it. Her ravening nails hit his back. He fell, holding back a raw scream.

Somehow he managed to flip, to hold off the fangs at arm's length. But now his *pukko* leaped from his hand, was lost in the shadow under the long trough. Ilmar screamed silent prayers as he felt the sideswipes the fangs made at his arms. Agony and sheer need pulled him half up on his feet.

He kicked out at the bitch's underbelly. When, momentarily, she moved back in agony, he leaped up

on the trough. Her heavy leap rocked the trough and
sent Ilmar plunging backwards. He half-turned in mid-
air, then, with an agonized groan of tortured muscles,
he contrived to dump the trough. On the hell-bitch.

The ice-cold dousing did what the kick had started.
She slunk away, whining and shivering.

But now, it seemed, his night's work with Louhi's
mindless killers was only well started. Flaming eyes and
exultant baying voices converged on the well-trough from
all directions.

Ilmar staggered back, conscious of bleeding pain from
many portions of his anatomy. And of a quiet nagging
despair, rising acid and sour in his throat.

"Here, Ilmar!" A soft urgent voice rang out above the
baying of the hounds. *"Run!"*

"Karina!"

His abrupt glance showed him the girl at the bake-
house, flinging what looked like great haunches of raw
meat from the open top-half of the dutch doorway.

He needed no engraved invitation. When he saw that
some of the dogs were diverted by her free lunch, others
slowed by indecision, he flung across the wan moon-
patch at a championship gallop. Never had his long legs
moved so fast.

The bottom half of door was ready to embrace him,
and so was Karina. She held him very close, then crooned
sobs over his hurts.

"You should have waited, Ilmar. I meant to signal
you—"

*"Perkele,* child! An Ussi watch would have helped."

He glanced out at the dogs and their early lunch
with a wide blink; first they were snarling and snapping
among themselves, then they shuddered on wobbling
legs and dropped.

"What did you do, Karina?"

"Green rat poison from the Castle kitchens. You should have waited for my signal."

"Never mind. Did you find a way to the Tower?"

"I think so. One of the stone masons had mentioned to the scrubbing wench he is wooing that—"

"Let's go!"

She nodded; Ilmar followed her lead along the shadowed fringe of the time-scarred Tower rearing into the fogs, to the acute angle where the Tower abutted the great front feasting hall, unused in a century or more. Karina halted before a wild tangle of dead-leaved vines.

"Here, I think."

Ilmar patted her shivering shoulder and grinned. "Take it easy, girl. If there is one, I'll find it." He groped his hands behind and among the wintering shrubs, seeking out crevices between the ancient stones. A silence like the surrender of eternity enveloped the shrouded courtyard. Nothing. Nothing. A tormented passage of breathless time, then his seeking fingers caught in an opening like a grooved cup. Ilmar forced his hand further into the cup and pulled with his full strength.

Unseen levers went into action. Silently the corner's stones sunk back. A narrow opening invited them into the tower's base.

Karina gasped. Ilmar felt her shiver against his shoulder.

"Why don't you go back? Even if the Witch finds out you helped me—and I don't make it—she won't hurt you. She likes your baking too much."

"Too late," Karina wailed. "Besides, now that I know there *is* someplace besides this dreadful island—I can't live here any longer. If you fail—" She clung fiercely.

"I *can't* fail, Karina! I understand. Shall we—?"

The girl's grip, leech-tight, as he preceded her up the long narrow twist of stone stairs, was some comfort in the musty cold black climb. The winding walls were so close together that Ilmar's shoulders wouldn't fit; he had to move sideways. When Karina's panting breath began to tear into sobs he halted, so that they could at least lean on the slimy stone and rest for a minute or two.

Rats scuttled across the high steps, squealing angrily at their impudent intrusion.

"We could use some of that arsenic," Ilmar said wryly.

"W-What about the Witch?" Karina's voice was hollow and strained. Her whole life had been a proving ground for terror of Louhi and her demon's powers. Back in her warm bake-house her Mistress was only a frightful name. Now, to be actually on the move against Louhi, was too much to face.

Ilmar understood all this. He wanted to tell her to go back to her ovens and her seed-cakes, yet—was there any going back? The hell-dogs were Louhi's pride and joy. She was bound to find out how they had died, torture it out of the girl if necessary, and even her proficiency as a baker for the greedy hag would not save her.

"We'll need something stronger than arsenic for Louhi," he said grimly.

"*What?*" Karina demanded. "You must have brought something with you that will kill her! Please tell me!"

Ilmar sighed. "I'm not a sorcerer, Karina. Right now I wish I was."

"Then—?"

"I'll have to play it by ear. Can you think of any weak spot in her witchery that might help?"

The girl shivered. "No-o. There isn't any!"

They moved up. Up. Up. Up. Ilmar's head pounded, dizzied by lack of oxygen in the narrow slot and the upspiraling. His inner ears screamed their loss of equilibrium. For a space of raw time he had to pull loose from

Karina's convulsive grip and plank both hands against the wall, while he retched up dry physical pain.

"It *can't* be much further!" the girl wailed.

Ilmar wondered vaguely in the maelstrom of his mind why Karina could take the everlasting spring-coil better than he.

"I don't *dare* be sick," she gasped. "If I let go of myself I'll fall, and never get up."

He found her hand and dragged her on. "As you said, there has got to be an end some place."

When it came, the foul-aired journey ended fast. Ilmar found himself plunging through thick draperies, then pinching his eyes and blinking out through an arched alcove into an amber-lit hall. Straight ahead was an ebony-black door, a high door fashioned out of alien angles and designed for others than only humans.

"I wonder," Ilmar murmured. "Is this—"

"Yes, Ilmar. This is the Witch's most secret chamber."

Something in her voice, something new, made Ilmar whirl sharply. Karina started to laugh. She rocked and danced with sudden-freed joy.

"Karina!"

She brushed by him with a small light dance step, laughing her gleeful chortle as if all of this were the finest of all sports. When she reached the black door she turned on him full-face and now Ilmar knew.

He knew and turned into solid rock for a large minute.

Karina was not Karina, after all. No.

She was the star-hag's nameless daughter.

# THE STAR MILL

## XIII

"WHAT THINK you of my demon's chick, Smith?"

"Don't get me started."

"Go right ahead," Louhi cackled. "Don't mind me. I've heard everything and done most."

Ilmar faced the Witch, a sorry rag of a hero, indeed. His tunic and his hide were torn by the dogs, and the chagrin behind the copper beard was of a twist to gladden Louhi's sunken eyes down to her lost soul.

The star-hag was seated to the rear of a half-round room on a black throne. A long slice of window in the stone allowed weak morning light to bleed in, and besides this there were two iron dragon lanthorns hanging to each side of her, making orange flame-shadows across her deep scarlet witch's robe and the horror she wore for a face. To one side was a cavern of slumbering fire where Koko dozed on heaps of yellow cushions.

Louhi relished the sight of Ilmar's ignominy, rocking back and forth among alien green furs. Her fur-trimmed robe fell about her hump and her crumpled-steel body in luxurious folds, jeweled claws scuttled out of voluminous sleeves; her time-blackened face was so squeezed and contorted by unspeakable sins that it was hardly human any more. Ilmar's first full look brought a deep gasp of physical pain. The condor's eyes were crimson at the edges and the pupils were blank holes pulling him down into her brain's bottomless pit.

"Beautiful, eh, son of Ilmarinen?"

Ilmar forced his eyes away from the Witch, to her daughter. It was a relief; but angry chagrin fired his high cheekbones. Yes. Louhi's daughter was beautiful. As beautiful as the sky-hag was hideous. Which seemed practically impossible.

113

The young witch preened for him. She danced lightly around the room, while the flame-tongues of the hanging dragons licked across her superb, voluptuous body. She kept changing like a chameleon. Now she was a blue-eyed brunette sheathed in soft green chiffons; now she was a big-breasted blonde in vivid gold that seemed to have been painted on; now an auburn beauty with a white cameo face and temptingly pursed red lips.

Now she was Karina.

"No, damn you!" Ilmar's throat tore the words out. "I don't believe it! You aren't really her!"

On her throne, Louhi cackled as she rocked. "Hiisi's chick can be anything!"

She went on and on, putting on other provocative bodies made more so by other dazzling costumes. She was Cleopatra. She was Helen. She was every man's secret dream, and the manner in which she danced and mocked with her beaded eyes told Ilmar she knew his, too. He blushed to match his beard and wrenched his look away. She was Circe, too, turning men into swine.

"No wonder Ilmarinen fashioned me the Sampo, eh?" Louhi cried. "No wonder! Yes, youth. I created my Hiisi's daughter for a lure and a trap. I sang this into her, to my purpose. All she knows is her nymphomaniac body and her insatiable pride in tempting and trapping men." She whispered coyly. "I'm just like all mothers, I guess. I want my little girl to be everything I'm not."

Her words told Ilmar how to deal with the nameless sexpot. He ignored her. To be ignored was the one thing she couldn't take. Louhi understood and bit her lip.

"Enough!" She lifted her snake-stick and pointed it at the girl. "Get out! You can have him later, when I'm through with him."

The girl's taunting laugh was a promise; he bent his head not to see her as she brushed past him and out of the chamber, but her perfume was so rapturously wicked that he reeled back a step or two and held his breath until she was gone.

"She knows better than to disobey me," the Witch grumbled. "I permit her these vanities. She served her purpose, getting you up here."

"She isn't the real Karina," Ilmar gritted.

The hag chuckled. "Not the one Koko first brought you to, the one who hid you in the loft. No. *She* is real enough. She is the best bakeress I have ever had, a genius with flour and milk and other goodies." She grimaced. "Hiisi knows my pleasures are few these days. What good is my sorcery if I have nobody here to use it on?" Brushing him up and down with her hell-windows eyes, she relaxed again and wriggled with comfortable anticipation.

"She killed your dogs," Ilmar said.

"My demon pets! Hardly! A minor potion to put them to sleep, no more. To keep you from killing any more of my beauties, damn you!" Her face blazed for his blood. "Never mind, the others will finish you off when I and my daughter are through with you."

"Do you think there's enough of me to go around?"

"We'll make you last, son of Ilmarinen. As for Karina, I admire the girl's spunk. Most of this generation of my slaves are worms."

"Did you really spare her cousin?"

"Don't be ridiculous. I couldn't have her commit suicide on me. She's too good a bakeress. And her body is strong; it will bear many children to serve me, better than the other spineless tarts." She scowled thoughtfully. "I think—yes—I think Tursas will have her first."

Ilmar's body stiffened; his muscles and nerves shot through with electricity.

"Tursas." The name conjured up monstrous visions of Aijo's Iku-Turso, still hiding from Ukko in the molten fires at the center of a small green planet.

"My dog keeper. He has earned her. He has served me faithfully. Tursas is big as a bull and most of the jellyfish among my Castle servants offer him but little in the way of specialized entertainment."

Ilmar tried, but he couldn't keep back all his horror and anguish for Karina. The chords in his neck crackled with it.

Louhi curved a smile.

"That upsets you, does it? You are in love with Karina?"

Ilmar grated a no.

"Ah? There's some milk-faced slut pining away for you back among the Vanhat? Why don't you tell me her name. As you know already, I have managed to move Pohyola and my Storm quite a way in that direction, and soon I shall divorce my island from it by a time trick. I don't mind telling you, son of Ilmarinen, that much of my sorcery concerns what I learned many thousands of lifetimes ago: that *Time* is an illusion. When one learns how to manipulate it, back and forth, one lives forever and outwits the bumbling technology of the Ussi with very little trouble. True, the inside-out Sampo has had me trapped, and it is an all-powerful thing. But I have been working on the problem here in my tower for centuries, now, and I am on the very brink of escaping from it. So I shall be visiting my old enemies, the Vanhat, and I would be glad to give your *rakas* the sad story of how you died." She added, maliciously, "Especially I will be glad to tell her how, in the end, you succumbed to my daughter's so very many charms.

Which you will, son of Ilmarinen. You will, before the dogs get you."

Ilmar shrugged off the chilling implications and sent his mind darting in all directions. First he must make an effort to save Karina; and the only way he could possibly even try was to get her up here to the Tower.

"There isn't anybody else," he told her carefully.

"*Niin?*" She sniffed at his statement from all angles. "I am thinking now about you and Karina. A spurt of new blood in my stockyard might help. . . ."

Cupidity leaked out of those eyeholes. This was the lately-human creature who refused to share a Star Mill of endless resource with anybody. The cosmic string-saver. To Louhi, her slaves were like her bullocks, her sheep, her hogs.

"When one lives forever one must look ahead," she mused.

Silence.

"What did you have in mind?"

"You know what I have in mind, son of Ilmarinen. You are not stupid. Keep this in your head at all times: I know your thoughts. I am way ahead of you and all of your futile race. I need new blood and before you die, you may as well contribute."

Ilmar locked his lips together, then he decided to grudge out what would get Karina to the Tower. "I I would never do it, if only because it would please you, Witch!"

"No?" She rattled her snake-stick on the side of her throne noisily. "Koko! Wake up, slugabed!"

From his fetal curl on the silken cushion, Koko yawned himself awake, tinkling the bells on his ruff.

"First put some wood on the fire, insect!"

"At once, Mistress."

Koko hopped like a mantis from his fluffy perch and

scampered to feed the slumbering red coals from the woodheap. The Witch's eyes were on him, so Ilmar sped a fast look in the direction of the elongated thicklip window. Mournful dawn was dragging its misty self through the opening. Escape by the window? Ilmar considered such a possibility, discarded it, remembering the long sheer drop. And the Sampo? Where was the perverted Mill?

Hopping to crouch at his Mistress' feet, Koko turned his gooseberry eyes on Ilmar, pointing like a child. "Who is he, Mistress? I never saw him before."

"Friend of Karina's."

"Oh!" Koko's round green face brightened; his ears vibrated with ingenuous happiness. "Cousin Toivo from over the mountain!"

Louhi rumbled in her throat. She gave the dwarf a rap with her snake-stick and turned to Ilmar. "See why I keep him around? For one thing, he is too stupid to fear me, and that's a diversion in itself. Another thing, his race is so needful of affection that they will strain their talents to the utmost to get even crumbs."

"Talents?"

Koko had the run of the Castle and the farmyard *in toto*. Was there something else? Did the hag have a reason for allowing Koko to wander at will?

"It's beginning to penetrate that copper-covered skull, I see."

"You mean it was Koko? But I—"

Louhi's cackle was shrill and triumphant. "Very well. It will amuse me to show you why Koko makes such an excellent spy." She rapped the dwarf-alien on his frizzy head again. "Assume the position, bug!"

Eager to be of service and thus gain a morsel of his Mistress' spurious affection, Koko folded up his grasshopper's legs on the green fur rug at the Witch's feet. It was a familiar ritual, plainly. Ilmar watched with fascinated repulsion at what happened now.

"Koko's race are shy tree-climbers, hard to tame as koalas. But they have one special talent."

She tapped Koko's odd ears several times with her stick. "Show me a remember, little bug!"

Koko's emaciated body went stiff, all but the ears. They began to vibrate at the tips like hummingbird wings. His round green eyes turned to milky clouds and while this happened, the ears shivered themselves into a gray-green blur.

Then a strangeness occurred. A kind of powder poured out of the dwarf's ears and made a three-dimensional cloud over his head. It was like cartoon talk. But it was pictures. A race of kaleidoscopic pictures, a montage of hodge-podge images, until Louhi got the ones she wanted and tapped his head to halt them.

Ilmar saw himself meeting Koko in the meadow, through Koko's bulbous eyes. He saw himself take Koko's hand and lead him down the cowpath. There was no need for words. Louhi had intuited the truth. Especially how Koko's eyes had unwittingly seen Karina's disbelief in a returned Cousin Toivo and how she had hastily sent Koko to fetch water. . . .

Back to life, Koko clapped his hands and tittered cretinic rapture in having pleased his Mistress. Nothing else mattered to his alien mind but this.

"I understand," Ilmar said. "Koko's your spy. The servants and warriors will react freely around him because he's so childish."

"You catch on fast." The sky-hag sneered. "I'm tempted to keep you around for a while, perhaps on some cushions at the other side of the fire, for balance."

Ilmar ground his teeth and tried to think nothing. Let her Witch's tongue wag. Let her revel in her triumph while he could batter and badger his mind into devising some way of making it less than complete.

"Koko!" cracked Louhi. "Fetch my breakfast! Make sure that Karina has not bittered my milk-cakes with her tears!"

Koko scampered off through the black doorway. Louhi's eyes were sharp, swift blades when they turned abruptly on Ilmar. She seemed to have tossed idle torment ramblings to one side and reached a pinpoint decision.

"Yes, I would like to keep you around. It would be amusing to have your blood mixed with my next crop of slaves, to extend my vengeance, as I have sworn by Hiisi to do to all of the Vanhat, past, present, and future. Still, it might lead to trouble in the end. You are of heroic blood. You are immune to many kinds of death. You proved that by escaping from my dogs the last time you blundered past the Storm. No. I must not linger about your punishment and death. You Vanhat heroes are a devious lot." She rattled her snake-stick loudly on the stones and screamed for her warrior guards. "Go! Find out if my dogs are awake! Breakfast is ready!"


## XIV

ILMAR's long string-like muscles tied themselves into knots while he waited for Louhi's beast-faces to return. To end up as dogfood was scarcely what destiny and the loom of his Vanhat ancestry had presaged for him, but it was beginning to look as if that sword-brand on his face was a misnomer, after all. While Louhi slopped up porridge and a black brew that steamed like coffee but smelled like toad-vomit, Ilmar paced and made a furtive try at drawing out the Flame Sword.

It wouldn't budge!

Fashioned for one thing only, it could not help him now. It concealed itself around his belt as if it didn't exist; it fooled Louhi into unawareness of its existence; still, what good was it if he never got the chance to use it?

"Where is that insect, Koko!" Louhi grumbled, lifting her black walnut face out of her porridge. "Where are my seed cakes?"

Ilmar's dour smile downtilted his lips, but he was grateful to discover that Louhi had a carnal weakness. Food greed. After all, the sorceress of Pohyola, consort of star demons, had human organs within that shrunken, ancient body. That they were kept functional by her tricks with time was neither here nor there. Her perverse being evolved from the same beginnings as the Vanhat.

His glance measured the round room; servants tending to the witch's cranky desires in and out of the black doorway told him something surprising. There were no other rooms on this level; things were trooped up for her from somewhere below. Where, then, was the Sampo?

The explanation struck Ilmar like a thunderclap.

*The Star Mill was further up.*

Ilmar idled over to the window. A look down sent his senses to spinning. The courtyard below was a toy-town with linsey-woolsey-clad ants scuttling about. He craned a careful look up. Purple fog shadowed the Tower's summit. As far as he could see there were no ladders, no projecting stones, only a smooth unscalable surface of black stone.

"Get away from that window!" Louhi snarled. "I won't have you flinging yourself out, I want you to feel the dogs' fangs gnawing your bones!"

Ilmar shrugged, moving toward her. "I was just wondering about the Sampo."

"Keep wondering, Redbeard."

He decided to try, anyway. "Rather than stay trapped in the Black Storm any longer, why not destroy it before it reduces the universe to rubble and spoils your fun?"

"There are other universes." She showed her toothless gums. "Other times."

"Still—"

"Still nothing, offspring of Ilmarinen! The Sampo cannot be destroyed. Once the power to convert *any* molecular matter into any other was started, the chain reaction is forever. Your ancestor and his meddling friends, Vainomoinen and Lemminkainen, found that out. Even I couldn't. The best I could do was to reverse its function. Now it must sit up there on its pedestal, gnawing away at the universe and all matter within it, until there's nothing left to disintegrate."

Her wild cackling turned his blood to ice.

The black door-curtain trembled and Koko burst in, out of breath and carrying a covered tray.

"About time," Louhi grumbled. "Bring me the cakes, bug!"

When the curtain billowed, Ilmar thought he caught a small glimpse of full blue skirt and white blouse. Louhi's sharp eyes were on the cakes and her demand for more of her unholy tea. At least it seemed so until she spit out, "Come in, Karina. I won't bite you. I won't even gum you. Come in and say goodbye to your Vanhat friend."

The girl stepped through the tremulous curtains, her blue eyes wide and fearful. Ilmar went to her, took her hand. Sight of him put back a hint of color to her cheeks.

"I thought you were dead!"

He put an arm around her, to keep her from dropping to the stones out of relief and horror.

"Soon," cackled the hag. "Soon, you stupid child." She chomped her cakes with noisy relish. "What brought you up here? Do you want to die with your hayloft lover?"

Karina's cheeks sprouted crimson flowers. "He's not my lover! I—I heard about the dogs and—" She looked at Ilmar passionately. "You were gone! I was afraid, but I had to know what happened. I made Koko bring me back with him." She faced the Witch with desperate courage. "I don't care what you do to me."

"Good!" Louhi mocked. "I have amusing plans for you, trull. But first you might enjoy watching Ilmarinen's son play games with my pets. That will be your punishment for not telling me about his arrival at once. For hiding him."

Koko was feeding the fire and fingering his long ears absently. His appendages began to quiver violently as Louhi vented her anger with Karina in an explosive tongue-lashing.

"You won't kill her, Mistress?" he begged. " 'Cause if you do we won't get any more of those nice cakes."

"Silence, bug. I shall simply take a page out of Ilmar's book and erase her memories of him, as he did yours. Come close to me, girl!"

An invisible demon's wire dragged Karina away from Ilmar toward Louhi's throne. Ilmar was on the point of disturbing the Witch's pattern of concentration, when another idea struck home. He moved across the room to Koko without sound.

"Koko!" he whispered into one of those more-than-ears, "we're all in peril of death from this Witch!"

"Not me?" he wailed.

"You, too! I can't explain it to you. You wouldn't understand. But you've got to help us!"

"Help?"

"You love Karina, don't you?"

Koko gaped, saucer-eyed, while the wheels in his oversize head meshed cogs and moved with ponderous effort.

"But—"

Behind them the Witch was aiming her mind at Karina, pruning away her memory of Ilmar very carefully, so that none of her baking talents would be disturbed. It was what she had done to Ilmar, not simple hypnotics but a straightening out of the convolutions of her brain. It occupied her fully, for a moment or two. He must use those moments well. . . .

"Koko," he said to the alien. "Assume the positon. Do like you do for your Mistress. Show me a remember!"

Koko's face screwed up in a painful demur, but Ilmar's hands on his long ears folded his mantis-legs to a kneel. Ilmar's eyes blazed his demand. *Ukko. Give me of your Power.*

"Now, Koko!"

The gooseberries blanked out and the powdery ions spurted out of Koko's ears. The balloon pictures were ragged and sketchy but there was one. . . .

"That's it, Koko! Where does the Witch go secretly when—"

Louhi's boiling scream shattered the rapport between Ilmar's driving demand and Koko's strange talent. Koko fell back in a moaning heap. Ilmar whirled to see Louhi tottering livid-faced off her carved throne, brushing past an immobilized Karina. Her eyes were wide gulfs of horror as she lifted her writhing snake-stick at Ilmar.

"Die, scum of Otava! *Die!*"

Ilmar snatched the lingering Power Thread Ukko had

loaned him before it could vanish; he tore his eyes away from the deathtrap leaping out from those windows to hell; he moved without thought, springing behind the Witch and pinning her meatless bones against him. The odor of her ophidian evil was overpowering but he thrust away his retching, his vertigo. This was the time for full belief in himself, in Ukko, in the cumulative essence that had branded him as born to one all-vital purpose. There was no time for anything else. Not for Koko. Not for Karina. Not for his own imperfect physical being. He must demand the Thread of Power, bind it to himself and to the sky-hag, use it, coalesce his spiritual self as the elder Vanhat had, with all that exists and use all that infinitude of power to keep Louhi at bay.

It was too much; but what he did manage was enough to propel the hag's grotesque physique to the window. A twist that snapped bone sent the serpent-stick hissing across the chamber.

Ilmar hoisted her, shrieking, to the stone ledge. A low fog-ridden wind plucked at her scarlet robe. Her shrieks changed to a long compelling wail aimed at her bizarre consorts brooding in the black fathomless reaches of space, but in a leap Ilmar was up on the ledge with her, clapping his hand over her mouth. They teethered there for a tangled moment, on the brink.

"None of your tricks, madam," Ilmar gritted. "I've got your mind in a net. Now—up the wall, please!"

Louhi's strangled moan was venom that stung his hand like fire. With one swift move he ripped a long tatter of gag from his torn tunic and rammed it in her mouth. Louhi's voice must be stilled as her mind had been snared, during that tick of time when she was over-confident and cut-powered from snipping off bits of Karina's memory. Ukko's power crackled around them like invisible thunder, to Ilmar's genetic claim on him,

but it was up to Ilmar to hold it fast. And that was
like holding quicksilver, like milking a goat into a sieve.
Louhi, Witch of all Witches, was fighting to free herself, and Ilmar would not be able to hold her for long.

His left hand held her wrists behind her, while his
right spun her to the sidewall and the brink. If they must
fall, it would be them both. He felt her bone-bag of
loose skin shudder with the prospect of annihilation; below them the whole of Hiisi's sky-island quaked. Was
this the end of such perfection of evil?

"Up!" Ilmar cried in her ear. "Climb up!"

She shook her head and hunched her hump to indi-
cate that there was no way to go up.

"Up, Witch! I saw it in Koko's remember. You
ought not to have let him see you scuttle out of this
window. Where else would you be going but to gloat
over your treasure? You yourself gave the first hint when
you said, 'up on its pedestal.' "

Louhi's moan was a scabrous prayer to unholy things,
but when Ilmar teetered her and himself half-off the
ledge she lashed loose a claw and grabbed. Where she
grabbed, a hairy black hand appeared, to clasp it. Up
she scuttled, like a scarlet demon's wing, up the ladder
of hairy hands. And Ilmar after, among, and with her.

It was a frantic pull, up into the purple fogs that forever shroud Pohyola like a hallmark of horror. Louhi
moaned and rattled her ossified bones to shrug herself
free from him, but Ilmar's grip and his voice whispering
in her ear that Ukko was still with him and it would be
them both that fell, kept her upclawing for the hirsute
rungs. Her hate would kill Ilmar but would kill her, too.
It was stalemate.

At last they were climbing over the serrated ramparts
and Ilmar found himself blinking up at the machine of
all-power, the rearranger of all matter, which Louhi's

meddlesome magic had twisted into a thing that only broke up all matter and fed on what it shattered.

Staring, Ilmar found it hard to believe. But the great whirling ball of rainbow colors was there, there in the center of the Tower's top on its black stone pedestal, hurling up its malignant and implacable power in a soot-black spiral into the void to destroy all that the universe had so painstakingly contrived for untold millenia.

Unbelief turned to awe.

"What is this wonderful, terrible thing? This thing that can uncreate and recreate—that can take the smallest particles of existence and change them into whatever its master wishes!"

Ilmar shivered and almost loosed his mind-clutch on the Witch. Ancestral guilt flogged him. What a fool Ilmarinen had been! What a consummate fool! Even in its original happier state the Sampo was a menace. Food. Clothes. All manner of luxury. *What then?* No. To possess the Sampo in any form was to become greater than a god. . . .

He must do it fast. He must not think on it.

NOW!

The rubied hilt of the Flame Sword leaped to his grasp this time, for within was Ilmarinen's blood and the essence of his time-stopped will to destroy what he had created. The sword flamed out like a glorious threshing whip; it sang across the mordant fog like all-things' ransom personified; it blazed with sunfire as it streaked out to catch the Star Mill in a spinning noose. Seeing the god's thing crumble and vanish shook Ilmar's soul so that his cells forgot to hang on to Louhi, forgot that he was the convergent apex of starpower. He had done what the painful foregathering of ancestral fumbling with genes had designed him for. It was over.

Overhead, Louhi's cackle mocked him. She had slipped

away while he was wonder-dazzled by the destruction of the Sampo. That cackle said: *We will meet again, puny dog of the Vanhat!*

Walking across the misted meadow, Ilmar holding Karina's hand and Karina holding Koko's, the dwarf observed, "That scar on your face is gone, Cousin Toivo."

Ilmar laughed down at the little alien with the gooseberry eyes and the remembering ears, wondering what Aino would say to such a foster-child after the wedding-feast was over.

"Where are we going, Cousin Toivo?" Karina asked.

"I'm not your—" Ilmar sighed. "Never mind. I'll fill you in after we get there."

"Where are we going?" Koko chortled.

"Through that Gate at the edge of the forest," Ilmar told them, thick-throated with joy to see his Valley once again.

"Good!" Koko cried. "I like picnics!"